Dear Romance Reader,

Welcome to a world of breathtaking passion and never-ending romance.

Welcome to *Precious Gem Romances.*

It is our pleasure to present *Precious Gem Romances,* a wonderful new line of romance books by some of America's best-loved authors. Let these thrilling historical and contemporary romances sweep you away to far-off times and places in stories that will dazzle your senses and melt your heart.

Sparkling with joy, laughter, and love, each *Precious Gem Romance* glows with all the passion and excitement you expect from the very best in romance. Offered at a great affordable price, these books are an irresistible value—and an essential addition to your romance collection. Tender love stories you will want to read again and again, *Precious Gem Romances* are books you will treasure forever.

Look for eight fabulous new *Precious Gem Romances* each month—available only at Wal★Mart.

Lynn Brown, Publisher

# FRIENDS AND LOVERS

## Marianne Evans

Zebra Books
Kensington Publishing Corp.

http://www.zebrabooks.com

To Steve—A friend and lover in the truest sense. I'm a writer, but
words alone can't express how grateful I am to have you in my life.
You never once doubted this day would come.
To Dan & Beth—You guys are the sparkle and spice in my life!
Thanks for being such great kids!
To Frank & Rhea DeSantis—Mom, dad, your support and never
failing encouragement gave me the strength I needed to
see this through. I love you both so much.
To my sisters of the scribe, The Critiquettes—Lisa Drummond, Nancy
Fraser, and Debbie Lampi. Thanks, guys, for sharing it all—
the laughs and tears, the successes and frustrations.
And, finally, to Kate Duffy & Kelly St. Clair—
For giving my dream wings.

ZEBRA BOOKS are published by

Kensington Publishing Corp.
850 Third Avenue
New York, NY 10022

Copyright © 1996 by Marianne Evans

All rights reserved. No part of this book may be reproduced
in any form or by any means without the prior written consent
of the Publisher, excepting brief quotes used in reviews.

If you purchased this book without a cover, you should be
aware that this book is stolen property. It was reported as "unsold and destroyed" to the Publisher and neither the Author
nor the Publisher has received any payment for this "stripped
book."

Zebra and the Z logo Reg. U.S. Pat. & TM Off.

First Printing: November, 1996
10 9 8 7 6 5 4 3 2 1

Printed in the United States of America

# One

"Jen, it's Mom. You better come to the hospital."

Jennifer Meyers took a sustaining breath of air, quickly tuned out the hubbub of *The Chicago Sentinel* sports department.

"Is it Dad?" she asked, her voice tight with emotion.

"Yes."

Nothing else was said. Nothing else was necessary. Jennifer didn't look left or right, didn't care that suddenly, with a single phone call, she had turned into nothing more than a robot, her feelings shunted aside as carelessly as a coat at spring time.

Through a haze she remembered to tell her boss she was leaving. He nodded, gave her arm a squeeze and murmured condolences, but his apologies pricked at her nerves. They weren't necessary. Not yet. There was always hope . . .

Until she got to the hospital.


"Hey, Mark!"

Just back from a late lunch, Mark Abington walked through the open space of the *Sentinel* sports department. He greeted one of his colleagues with a wave, noticing that the desk directly in front of his office was empty. Mark frowned.

"Where's Jen?" he asked, checking in with his chief editor, Tom Brewer. Uncharacteristically, his boss sat idle behind his desk, looking depressed as he thumbed through a pile of wire copy.

Tom's eyes said it all, even before he reported. "The hospital. You just missed her."

Mark's mood did an immediate down turn. He nodded and went to his office. For the next half hour he went through the motions of writing; he plugged in his lap top computer, set it up on his desk and began to draft his daily column. When words failed him, he took off his suit jacket, rolled up his shirt sleeves, then raked his hair back with his fingers a few times.

Nothing worked. The usual, mundane habits he had cultivated through the years to spur on his muse completely failed him today. And he knew precisely why. Jennifer. Her father had been sick for months. Following a stroke, her father had been hospitalized for nearly a week now. Mark couldn't keep his mind off her, and knew concentration was a lost cause, so he packed it in for the moment, knowing he'd accomplish nothing until he saw her.

"Tom," he said in passing, "I'm going to University Hospital. I'll transmit my column before nine o'clock tonight so don't worry about my space in the morning edition."

Mark knew he didn't have to wait for approval. He carried enough clout at the paper that he could shift his schedule like this, as long as his work was done—and done well.

For now, he let himself concentrate on Jennifer. She would need comforting, and nothing would keep him from helping Jennifer if she needed it.


At the hospital, Mark wasn't sure where to go, so he asked the receptionist in the lobby of the hospital about Daniel Meyers. When he was directed to I.C.U., he could feel a sudden and oppressive weight start to settle on his shoulders. He knew Jennifer had feared another set back to her father's health, and the news that he had been transferred to Intensive Care robbed Mark of what little hope he felt.

He took an elevator to the fifth floor. Searching for the room, he found Jennifer's mom pacing the aisleway in front of the nurse's station.

"Mrs. Meyers?" They had only met once before, at Jennifer's 25th birthday party nearly a year ago, so he could bring himself to call her Helen. She looked haggard, her hair mussed, her eyes puffy and red. Maybe it was the pervasive aroma of antiseptic, or the pallid gray lighting of the hallway in, but he got bad vibes immediately.

"Mark, it's good to see you." She already sounded grief-stricken and numb.

"Mrs. Meyers . . . ?" he asked, urgency in his tone. "Is everything all right?"

She nodded toward a nearby door and Mark followed the direction of her gaze. As he moved away, Jennifer's mom took hold of his arm and held him in place.

"He passed away." Her voice wavered. "She got here about ten minutes afterward. She's . . . .well . . . she's very upset . . ."

He didn't wait to hear more.

Quietly, schooling as much calm into his demeanor as possible, Mark entered the small, glassed-in room. Immediately he came aware of an eerie silence. There was no humming machinery, no blipping heart monitor or thumping respirator. Not anymore. He blinked hard to ease the stinging dryness in his eyes.

Jennifer's back was to him. Sitting in a chair that had been positioned next to the bed, she held her father's hand. Her shoulders shook, but her tears were silent. Oddly that moved him all the more.

He was about to touch her back, and alert her to his presence when the glitter of an amethyst and diamond ring on Jennifer's right hand caught his eye. His. Hers, actually. Well, *theirs*. He had given her the ring, her birthstone, as a gift of friendship about two months ago . . .

*"Oh! . . . Lord, Mark! I can't possibly . . ." Ignoring the dinner they shared at Mark's home, she lifted the ring box reverently from the table top, tilting it so the amethyst stone could catch the light. "Is it ever beautiful!" Determinedly she looked away, trying to ignore the beauty of the piece. "I can't accept this!"*

*Nevertheless, she removed the ring from its velvet and silk box, examining it as the two side diamonds caught fire with light. It wasn't a large ring, but the gold band and emerald cut stone was so beautiful it made her sigh.*

*"You can accept it and you damn well better accept it because I have no intention of returning that ring, Face. You didn't get a dime for all the hours of help you gave me putting together my book."*

*The project, a biography about Phil Jackson and his Championship season with the Chicago Bulls, had already won Mark wide acclaim throughout the nation—most particularly in his home state of Illinois.*

*Immediately after getting approval to write the book, he had en-*

listed Jennifer's help. Together they had done research, interviewed people, and prepared a manuscript. More than anything else, the book about Jackson and the success of seeing it on bookshelves had solidified a strong bond of friendship between them.

She studied the ring once more, a look of longing on her face. She was tempted, Mark knew. Very tempted.

"I helped you willingly," she went on to say. "It was a labor of love. Really. You didn't have to..."

"It went number one in Illinois today," he reported, pride in his voice.

With a squeal of delight, Jennifer launched herself into his arms. 'Number one?' He nodded, laughed as he enjoyed her enthusiasm. 'Mark! That's great! I'm so happy for you!'

'Then be happy for yourself, too, Face. I couldn't have written the book without your help. Celebrate by keeping this ring—as a reminder. It would mean a lot to me. Enjoy, that's all I ask.'

With a little help, the ring went on her finger.

It hadn't been off since.

"Hello, Face," he whispered gently.

She spun toward him. Her cheeks were wet with tears, her eyes, like her mom's, were red and glassy. "Mark..." She didn't as much speak his name as breath it. Slowly she stood. "God am I glad to see you."

"I'm so sorry, Jen."

For the time being she didn't try to form words but stepped into his open arms and laid her head on his shoulder. He swayed, rubbing her back with a light touch.

"If there's anything I can do..." he offered, not knowing what else to say.

"You're doing it," she murmured. Overcome by tears she added, "I got here too late, Mark. I didn't get to say good bye to him." After a shaky sob she said, "I feel sick inside."

They stood together in silent support, the quiet of the room unbroken until Jennifer's mom walked in.

"Stacy's back, Jen. I'm going home. There's a lot to do. I've got to make arrangements, and there's the family to contact..." Her voice sounded husky and rough from crying. "Are you coming?"

Jennifer glanced from Mark to her mom then back again. "If it's okay, I'll meet up with you and sis' later on."

"That's fine. Call me later." She looked toward the bed where her husband still lay. Distractedly she reached into the purse at her side and pulled out a white prescription slip. She handed it to her daughter. "Don't forget to get this filled, Jennifer, and don't stay here long."

"Listen to her," Mark advised, taking Jennifer's hand. "Matter of fact, I'll see to that now." Leading her from the room, Mark let go of her hand and put his arm around her waist. "Come on."

"McDonald's."

Mark chuckled lowly. "I should have known."

"A chocolate shake," Jennifer elaborated dully.

Her eyes were large and vulnerable. "No shocker there, either." He gave her an affectionate look. "You're a cheap lunch date, Meyers."

"Count your blessings," she replied absently, staring out the window of Mark's car as they drove through the streets of downtown Chicago. Passing the headquarters of the *Sentinel* prompted her to say, "You should be at work."

He pushed that idea aside with a shake of his head. "I should be right where I am, so be quiet." Mark awaited the rejoinder that normally would have followed, but Jennifer didn't oblige. Not this time.

"It's weird, you know."

"What's that?" To Mark, she seemed dazed and blank.

"I was writing a story on last night's high school basketball results. Then Mom called. It's weird how quickly your stomach can turn upside down and your whole life changes. Sometimes it doesn't take much. Just a phone call."

Reaching across the arm rest of the seat he took her hand and held it firm. Jennifer tilted her head, watching Mark as he navigated the traffic patterns around Michigan Avenue.

Thick and wavy, his dark brown hair was cut short, framing the squared lines of his face in well-styled layers. Right now, though, his hair had been tussled, probably pushed back by anxious fingers once he had heard about her father.

Jennifer smiled, wanting to smooth her fingers against his cheek, take away all the concern. Mark, she knew, got very wrapped up in the concerns of people he cared for. As evidence, the corners of his almond colored eyes were engraved by a faint spray of lines that were more pronounced now than usual. He bore quite a responsibility at the *Sentinel,* being their chief sports reporter at a mere 31 years of age. But talent like his, she believed, couldn't be denied. He had already won more national and local sports writing awards than could be easily counted, but she knew him well enough to realize the acclaim didn't matter, only the joy his writing gave him.

They stopped at McDonald's. Although he had already eaten, Mark ordered a fish sandwich and a cup of coffee while Jennifer ordered nothing but the shake.

"Not even french fries?" he asked, trying hard to tempt her appetite. She shook her head. "Get something, Face, you must be hungry . . . and it's my treat."

"The shake is enough for now," she insisted.

Mark paid for the food and they sat at a booth to eat. Noise swirled, a backdrop full of conversations, the occasional bang of cookware, ordinary, everyday sounds that Jennifer registered on one level, tuned out on another. She barely spoke, didn't really see anything she looked at as she sipped her shake.

Fidgeting with a plastic fork, Mark was quiet as well, but he kept his focus on Jennifer. Memories flooded through him. They had only known each other for a few months when she asked an innocent question about his pet name for her . . .

*"Why do you call me 'Face' all the time?"*

*"Look in a mirror." he answered, sorting through a pile of work on his desk, "then you won't need to ask."*

*She sat across from him and Mark paused, studying her carefully. Jennifer's beauty wasn't of the variety found on modeling runways, but it was there, and strongly, none the less. Permed, chin length hair of dark brown was thick and softly styled around her face. Average height and slender, she tended to favor traditional, professional looking outfits—skirts and blouses, blazers, suits—yet she wore them all with flair.*

*"Mark. I'm serious!"*

*"So am I!" he retorted.*

*"Answer my question, or I'll call you Marcus Allen for the rest of your life."*

*"Hummm . . . good threat." There was a pause while he looked into her eyes. "I call you Face because you're beautiful, first of all, and secondly, everything about you is revealed in your face." He*

*elaborated with a description that made Jennifer smile.* "Your eyes are innocent and caring, your mouth is a perpetual smile . . . happiness in a curve . . . and there's softness in your face. Gentleness. All that you are is right there. Out in the open. In your face, Face."

Jennifer rolled her eyes with a groan, lobbing a paper wad at her colleague. "Spoken like a man who writes for a living. You certainly have a way with words."

Mark shook free of the memories, wishing he could ease her pain. But time, he knew, would be the only antidote for that.

"Let's get out of here," he said, knowing he sounded abrupt.

Jennifer looked at him, a bewildered expression on her face. As though beyond comprehending his mood swing, she simply shrugged. "Okay. I'm ready to go home I guess."

"That's not what I mean, Jen. I don't want to get rid of you. Let's go to my place. It's quiet there. We can talk."

She clenched her jaw, mumbling, "I don't really feel like talking."

"Fine then, we won't talk. We can sit around and listen to music instead." They stood in unison, but Jennifer found herself brought up short when Mark stood in her way, ever protective. "By the way," he said, "I didn't miss that prescription order your mom gave you. What's it for?"

"Nothing!" Turning her back on him, she adjusted her purse strap on her shoulder.

"Jennifer!"

"It's for a sedative that I have no intention of taking. End of disc . . ."

Mark pulled her forward. "First stop, the drug store."

Wordlessly, using nothing more than her eyes, Jennifer pleaded with him to let the topic rest. Mark ignored her.


"I love Miles Davis," Jennifer sighed. "He's great."

Soothed by the lilting sound of jazz trumpet music that currently played on his stereo, Mark leaned his head back on the couch.

Several hours had passed since their stop at McDonald's, and Jennifer desperately wanted a glass of the Chablis wine she had spied in Mark's refrigerator.

"I still think you're a rotten host," she griped halfheartedly. "All I wanted is a little bit of wine."

"No way. I'm not giving you any alcohol. You're going to be taking a sedative later and alcohol and valium don't mix."

She winced, her actions a silent protest. "I hate that word."

"What word is that?"

"Valium. It's so weak sounding, you know? There are people at work who get stressed out and they say, 'I wish I had valium,' or 'I wish I had a valium dispenser . . . I'd have it empty by now.' " Jennifer shook her head, definitive on the matter. "I *don't* need the help of drugs."

Mark didn't buy a word of her speech. "Good Lord, Jen, do you realize how stubborn that sounds? You just lost your father. Taking a sedative doesn't mean you're weak and you know it."

She smirked, but Mark found no fault with her sullen attitude. Instead, he put an arm around her shoulders to bring her close.

Laying her head against his chest, Jennifer felt at once secure, calm, and comforted. Reluctantly she looked at the dial of her watch, knowing it was getting late. She truly hated to leave. "I should be going home."

Mark's hold on her tightened and he looked into her face. "You checked in with your mom earlier. What did she have to say? Are you going to her house tonight?"

"No. She's got Stacy, and my aunt is with her, too. She's got a full house, and arrangements to take care of for the funeral. I figured on going back to my place."

Mark straightened, meeting her tired eyes squarely. "You *are not* going to be alone tonight. If you've got no plans to be with your mom then stay here."

Jennifer's mouth quirked. "You just want to make sure I take my grog medicine."

"No."

"Yes."

Mark had the good grace to look sheepish for a moment. "Okay, okay, guilty as charged. But I don't want you to be alone. Stay with me, Face. I'd enjoy your company."

Beside him, Jennifer stretched. "Likewise. But if your offer is serious, I'm afraid I won't be much fun. I'm starting to shut down, Mark. I can feel it all setting in. I'm ready for bed."

"The numbness is wearing off. When it does, you're going to need the valium to make things a little easier. Agreed?"

"Agreed," she surrendered, eyeing the couch. "I'll stay out here, if you don't mind an early night."

Clucking his tongue, Mark pulled her gently to her feet. "Follow me."

"Like I have a choice . . ."

He took her upstairs, to his bedroom. Pointing toward an adjoining bathroom, he handed her a Chicago Bears jersey to wear. "Change into this." He folded back the beige and brown striped comforter of his bed. "Then climb in."

Jennifer was aghast. "You don't have to give up your room. I'll sleep on the couch."

"You'll sleep," he told her firmly, "right here, and I'll join you when I'm done with tomorrow's column." She looked down at the floor and Mark stuffed his hands into the pockets of his slacks. "Hey, Face, there's nothing lurid being offered here. Remember who you're with. This is strictly platonic." Serious in expression and tone, Mark moved toward her and took hold of Jennifer's hands. "I want to be here for you tonight. Having someone next to you might help you feel less alone."

Actually, Mark was right, and she trusted him implicitly. After all, he was one of her best friends. Besides, the thought of trying to sleep, alone, in a dark room, filled her with dread.

"Are you sure this is okay?" she asked softly. Jennifer looked into his eyes and saw nothing there that caused her to doubt his sincerity. He wanted to take care of her and be a friend. Typical Mark Abington.

"I'm sure."

"Besides," she said ruefully, walking to the bathroom, "I'll soon be unconscious. I'd be no fun anyway."

"Gee," Mark teased, reconsidering, "I hadn't thought of that. Cancel the whole deal then. The couch awaits."

"Creep."

She closed the door to change and had to admit, getting out of her work clothes felt wonderful. The jersey Mark had loaned her fit loosely, the way she liked sleep wear to fit, and it was so long that it skimmed her knees.

Mark waited next to the bed when she reentered his room. For a moment, since she had never seen his bedroom before, Jennifer looked around, liking the way he had decorated it. There were dark wood furnishings, recessed, brass-rimmed lights, thick, cream carpeting, and horizontal blinds that covered a large window to her right. Everything here spoke of comfort and understated luxury.

"You're sure I'm not interfering?" she asked again.

"Positive," he assured, gesturing toward the side of the bed where he stood. "Get to sleep."

She climbed in, pulled the blankets over her body, and it seemed like Mark was about to leave. Jennifer took hold of his hand, feeling cold all of a sudden. "Hang around for a while, okay? Until I fall asleep?"

"Sure, Face."

She moved toward the center of the bed so he could sit next to her. Leaning on his forearm, Mark drew her into the crook of his shoulder and placed a kiss on her forehead.

He didn't realize she was crying until he felt warm drops of water hit and spread against the material of his shirt.

"Jen?"

"Sorry," she mumbled, burying her face against him with a laden sigh. "I'm getting really tired."

"Don't fight it. Relax." He quirked a finger beneath her chin and drew her glittering eyes up to his. "If you feel like crying, then cry."

But she didn't. Not much, anyway. Jennifer closed her eyes, feeling his calm strength seep through her body. Never had she felt so comforted as she did at that moment, lying in Mark's arms. Restive at last, Jennifer dozed while he rubbed her back and the sedative took effect.

Her breathing evened out, becoming deep and smooth. Mark continued to hold her though, and he thought of the woman he held in his arms. They had seen each other through a lot during the two years that they'd been friends.

*"Gwynn's leaving."*

*Deliberate and purposeful, Jennifer set her yellow legal pad across her lap. She had been taking notes on a White Sox press conference Mark had attended just hours ago so she could write a sidebar. Now, seated next to him in his office, she ignored that task.*

*"New York?" Jennifer asked, knowing the situation full well.*

*"New York," he affirmed in a hurt tone.*

*"I'm sorry, Mark. Really sorry. When did you find out for sure?"*

*"Today. We had lunch together."*

*"Did you let her know how you feel?" Jennifer asked, leaning*

*forward to emphasize her next statement. "If you want her to stay, if you want a relationship with her, then you've got to let her know."*

*"Jen, she's as committed to her career as I am. She wouldn't change her plans any more than I would. The five o'clock anchor job is a great offer, a promotion. I can't ask her to give that up for me."*

*Silence fell between them for a time. "You could always go to New York."*

*But the thought seemed abhorrent to her, and Mark disliked the notion just as much. "Jen, I've got friends here, a great job, and I'm the high guy on the totem pole. Yes, I could get a job in New York, but I wouldn't be happy there, I enjoy working in Chicago."*

*"If you love her," Jennifer urged. "then talk to her. Let her know it, and at least consider your options. You seemed crazy about her, and vise versa. Don't let her get away unless you're sure it won't work."*

Next to Mark, Jennifer moved, settling into a deeper sleep. A year ago, his girlfriend Gwynn Aldridge had gone to New York. In truth, after the initial loneliness evaporated, Mark realized they had both done the best thing. Still, he found it odd that thoughts of Gwynn would crop up while he held Jennifer, easing her to sleep like a brother.

Soon he retraced his path to the living room and set up his portable computer, finishing his column for tomorrow's edition of the *Sentinel*. After transmitting it to the paper, Mark changed for bed and slid gingerly into the empty space next to Jennifer. She barely stirred at the movement. Mark stretched out next to her and brought her close, enjoying how warm she felt. Wrapping his arm lightly around her waist, he fell asleep within seconds.

"Jen, I'm leaving. Jen . . . ?"

Grumbling, her head feeling like it had been stuffed with cotton and grit, Jennifer turned toward the sound of Mark's voice. Focusing her vision with effort she saw that he stood next to the bed, dressed impeccably in a suit for work, awaiting her answer.

"What time is it?"

Mark grinned at her question. "You don't want to know."

"That early, huh?"

"Yep."

Her eyes stung, and she still felt incredibly tired. Dim light, from a crack in the bathroom doorway, was the only illumination in the room. The subtle, tantalizing aroma of his cologne found its way into her consciousness, alerting her senses.

"It's un-Godly to make a person do sportscasts this early in the morning on a stupid radio station."

"Tell me about it," Mark agreed with humor. "If the station weren't just half a mile away, there's no way I'd haul myself out of bed every morning this early."

Jennifer laid still for a time, quietly, before she said, "Tell Kevin hello. Let him . . ." She choked on her words and coughed to cover it up. "Let him know what happened, okay?"

Leaning over her, Mark pulled back a strand of hair from Jennifer's face and kissed her cheek. "You bet, Face." He straightened. "Stay put for a few hours and have breakfast. I'll call you later."

"All right. And . . . thanks for everything."


At 6:45 in the morning, the parking lot of the radio station was nearly empty. Mark locked his car and walked inside, taking an elevator to the second floor of the high-rise office building. He went directly to the broadcast studio.

"Hi, Mark!"

Mark started to reply to the greeting of Kevin Owens, the morning-drive D.J. of WCIO, then stopped short. "Hey, Kevin, got a minute?"

"Always."

Mark pulled him aside, into as quiet a corner as possible considering the half dozen people who made up Kevin's morning show. As ever, the studio was crowded, its four walls completely covered by posters, art from album covers, and promotional stickers. "Kevin, Jennifer's father passed away yesterday."

Shaken, he stared into Mark's face for a moment, absorbing the news. "How is she?"

The gruffness behind that question wasn't lost on Mark, and he found himself feeling irritated. "Fine, I guess, all things considered. She wanted me to let you know."

Kevin looked away, returned to his mike and started sorting

through a pile of compact discs. Boisterous laughter filled the air, bawdy jokes, too. Mark ignored the clamor, wanting to give his friend and colleague his complete attention.

"Was it a stroke?" Kevin asked at length.

Mark sat next to him. "Yes. The after effects of a stroke, to be more specific. She's hurting. *Again.*"

Kevin flinched at the way Mark emphasized the word. Checking the length of time left on the song that currently played, Kevin shrugged. "I can imagine. I feel awful for her."

"Look, she's your *ex*-fiancee, granted, but have some compassion. Get in touch with her and tell her that yourself. She could use your support."

"No way, man," Kevin replied in a panic. "Nothing against Jen but I can't do that. Not after what happened between us."

Mark didn't back off. He glared, saying tightly, "You feel that guilty, huh?"

"What if I do?" Kevin barked.

"I'd say *good. I'm glad.* At least guilt would prove you have a conscience."

Damned if that isn't the truth, Mark thought bitterly. Kevin and Jennifer had been engaged for nearly three months when a new staff member at the radio station . . . a bewitching, chic looking red head named Brenda . . . had set her sights on Kevin. Brenda's arrival splintered the relationship and Mark felt bad about that because he had introduced Kevin and Jennifer, hoping two of his closest friends would hit it off.

"Don't push me," Kevin warned.

"I'm not pushing, I'm stating facts." Mark nudged him in the arm, just hard enough to get Kevin to spare him a guilt laden look. "Give her a call. Get in touch with her."

The song ended. Without comment, Kevin resumed his show, bantering with the members of his crew. Mark walked out of the studio and went to the newsroom where he reviewed wire reports and typed up five minutes worth of script for his daily, morning sports show.

Automatically, Jennifer clicked on a radio that was nestled into the corner of a counter in Mark's kitchen. As usual she listened to

Kevin's show, but for the first time in the six months since their break-up, she didn't feel anything at all inside when she heard his voice. No pain, no betrayal, and no loneliness.

She felt pleased to discover that Mark was a fellow breakfast lover. Opening cupboards and exploring his pantry Jennifer found rolls, muffins, and croissants. Coffee had already been brewed and still steamed in the pot. She poured herself a mug full and dined on croissants and jam, waking up the way she most enjoyed . . . slowly.

But a rough day faced her. Thoughts of her father and the funeral to come kept her from being content. After last night though, and the way Mark had taken care of her, Jennifer felt much better equipped to handle it all.

# Two

The white handkerchief Jennifer clenched tightly in her fist was moist with tears. At the head of the warmly-lit parlour, her father lay in state. All day long people had ebbed and flowed through the room, murmuring condolences and assurances of support, commending Jennifer on her strength and poise.

Each time she heard the compliments, though, she felt like withering. Strength? Inside she felt like crumbling, the tremble of her over-wrought body controlled by only the barest of threads.

She worked the scalloped edge of the kerchief between her fingers, watching the movement with an odd sort of detachment. A group of people walked through the doorway of the parlour. Numbly, Jennifer looked up, mustering a smile of welcome for a group of people from the *Sentinel*.

Kylie Masterson, a fellow sports writer, took Jennifer's hands first, drawing her into a close hug. Unusually sedate, Kylie kept silent, though she stayed right at Jennifer's side as she greeted fellow colleagues and thanked them for the lovely bouquet of roses they had sent.

In truth, however, Jennifer wondered if she'd ever escape the smell of flowers, have them symbolize beauty, life and sweetness again instead of reminding her of tragedy.

At length, after greeting Jennifer's mom and sister, Kylie took Jennifer's hand once more and led her to a row of chairs.

As expected, Kylie behaved in a protective way, ordering, "Sit. You deserve a break."

Jennifer mumbled something she immediately forgot, feeling that odd numbness and distance from reality again.

But Kylie understood. "I don't want to try to talk right now, Jen," she said softly, "I know this is an awful, hazy time for you, but I hope you'll take time off from work. Relax and *recover*. Don't forget, I'm as close as a phone call."

Giving her friend a heartfelt smile, Jennifer nodded. "I know you are, Kylie. Thanks."

From behind, a pair of hands came to rest on Jennifer's shoulders. Inadvertently her body tensed with surprise and she turned, looking straight up into the solemn, uncertain face of Kevin Owens.

Lanky, fair of coloring and complexion, Kevin normally possessed a charming way of dealing with people that set them promptly at ease. But now he seemed decidedly uncomfortable. Thick blonde hair fell nearly to his shoulders. Nervously he shifted from foot to foot, his pale blue eyes focusing on Jennifer then moving quickly away.

Her interest by-passed Kevin, though, to take in the man standing next to him. Mark. Relief swept through her body in soothing waves, so potent it was palpable. Everything would be all right now. Mark was here, on stand by, ready to lend his support.

She stood in a smooth movement, Kylie temporarily forgotten as Jennifer faced the two men. "Hello, Kevin. I'm glad you're here."

He licked his lips, seeming tentative about being near her, which softened Jennifer's heart. Leaning toward him, she kissed his cheek. Tears sprang to her eyes for the umpteenth time.

"I'm real sorry, Jen," Kevin said lowly, looking more at the floor than her. "I thought a lot of your dad." His head came up as Jennifer's mom approached. "I hope you don't mind my being here, but I wanted you to know I care."

He stammered then, and Jennifer touched his face, a wan smile playing on her lips. "Of course I don't mind. This means a lot to me."

Silent, Mark watched them, affected by her sensitivity toward Kevin's discomfort. Yet he felt put-off as well. Why was she treating him so generously? Kevin had taken her heart and cut it to ribbons. *Hey,* he felt like saying, *I'm the one who was there for you. I'm the one who offered you refuge. Why are you being so damned kind to Kevin?*

Just as quickly, Mark regretted those thoughts. God he was being selfish. After all, who was he to question Jennifer's motives? She had been *engaged* to Kevin at one time.

That piece of reasoning, however, didn't do a thing to help. He felt no less resentful.

In passing, as she left to greet other visitors, Jennifer gave Mark's arm a tight squeeze and he worked hard at trying not to feel slighted. Scanning the room, he saw Tom Brewer, Kylie Masterson, and other employees of the *Sentinel* sports department. He moved to join them, but Mark's attention side-stepped when he watched Jennifer move through cliques of people.

Beneath the linen fabric of her black, peplum suit jacket, her shoulders looked tiny and frail. The matching slim-cut skirt she wore, her plain leather pumps and the single strand of pearls around her neck all painted a sorrowful picture.

Studying Jennifer while she accepted hugs and comforting words, seeing her reach out to others, stirred Mark and made him feel proud of her.

He stood quietly for the longest time, alone and uninterrupted, content to remain apart from everyone and simply watch her.

Bone tired, Jennifer longed for an escape hatch that would slip her away to sweet oblivion. She didn't want to struggle anymore, or maintain composure. Swollen and sore, her eyes burned. Her body literally ached for an end to this miserable day. Bravely though, she turned to survey the room, and make sure she hadn't neglected anyone.

She found Mark.

Leaning against a wing-back chair, he stood apart from the crowd, his gaze on her exclusively. He looked so strong, so invincibly solid. Her heart took him in by degrees that balmed her numb spirit. A double breasted suit of requisite somber color didn't diminish the compelling power of Mark's aura. His life force comforted her, assured her soul of better days to come.

Finally, she thought, I can be with the one person I need the most right now.

Mark watched her walk toward him and every muscle in his body went still. He felt her tenderness with stunning clarity. *Jennifer,* he thought, *let me be the one to help you. Don't reach out to others. You have me.*

The thought was possessive, true enough, but Mark alone knew her well enough to detect Jennifer's extreme vulnerability, despite her faultless demeanor toward those who shared her grief. He knew her best, therefore he felt honor bound to be her safeguard.

She didn't say a word as she stepped up to him. There was nothing inside her now that words could easily express. Looking into his eyes, she nodded toward the entrance of the room, beyond which was a lobby full of private seating areas.

Taking Jennifer's hand, Mark walked her slowly away from the oppressive, if loving, group of family and friends.

In private, she turned to him, her eyes shining.

"Would you mind holding me for a few minutes? I need to feel sheltered right now."

Mark had already drawn her close, wrapping both arms snugly around her waist. "You bet, Face."

Emotions made her feel weak-kneed. Love and sadness pooled, down deep in her stomach, releasing with her tears as she silently surrendered to grief.

Surprisingly, she discovered warmth was left behind as she snuggled more comfortably into his arms. Beneath her hand she felt the sure, steady beat of his heart, the firm, solid texture of his body. Comfort. Blessed, blessed comfort. Desolation didn't hold nearly as much power over her now.

Mark lowered his head, meaning to kiss her cheek, and came upon the spicy remnants of her perfume. An emotion, undefinable and foreign, swept through him in that instant, making his pulse rate leap. Keeping a tight hold of Jennifer's small, taut frame, he stopped short of a kiss and fingered her hair.

"Are you going to be all right, Face? You could probably use a break."

"No."

He knew that tone well. Don't even argue the point, she seemed to say. The case is closed.

"It wouldn't take you long to eat a meal," he encouraged.

Her eyes lifted to his. "My family is getting together for dinner after the visitation is over. Could you come with us?"

There was no way on earth he could deny her shimmering eyes, or the pleading look on her face. Keeping an arm around her waist, Mark nodded, reaching up with a fingertip to stroke the pale skin of her jaw and chin. "You bet, Jen."

From the corner of his eye, Mark saw Kevin Owens pass through the doorway of the parlour, ready to leave. Mark detected the look of puzzlement that crossed Kevin's face when he saw the two of them together.

Placing a brief kiss on Jennifer's cheek, he whispered, "Wait for me here. I'll be right back."

He followed Kevin out to the parking lot.

"Go ahead and take off," Mark advised. "I'm going to hang around for a while. Jen asked me to join her family for dinner and I accepted. I'll get a ride home from her."

"Suit yourself, pal."

Ice could have formed on the man's breath, his mood was so chilly. "What's wrong?"

"I'm just confused is all."

"About what?"

At the door of his car, Kevin turned on Mark. "What's going on between you and Jennifer?"

"Comforting, Kevin. Comforting."

He didn't buy that for a second, though, and Kevin gave his friend a derisive snort. "Oh. *Comforting.*"

"Don't give me this jealousy act. Considering past history, it makes you look like an idiot."

"Screw you!"

Mark yanked hard on Kevin's arm. "Cut the hostility! Jennifer and I have been good friends for a long time. You know this. Why so bitter all of a sudden? Could you suddenly be realizing what you've lost?"

That pierced, and rankled. As intended. All of a sudden it seemed Kevin had a thorn in his side about Jennifer. Why? Mark wondered.

"You looked a damn site more than just *friendly* in there, Abington."

"So what? Even if we were more than friends, Kevin, what in *hell* would that matter to *you?* You dropped her like dead weight once you caught sight of Brenda. That was cruel. Cruel and vicious."

The words had never been spoken aloud between them. Never had Mark broached the delicate subject of Kevin's break-up with Jennifer because of the relationship the three of them had shared. Besides, Mark was good friends with Kevin. They had gone to college together and even been roommates. Nevertheless, he felt guilty about what Jennifer had gone through. He felt responsible to a degree for Jennifer's heart break because he had not only introduced her to Kevin, but encouraged the relationship.

For the sake of friendship, when Mark looked into Kevin's angry eyes, he almost wished he had kept his mouth shut. Almost, but not quite. Kevin was acting like a jealous boyfriend, and Mark felt determined to guard Jennifer. Kevin had shattered her life without a hint of remorse . . . until now. That wouldn't happen again if Mark had any say in the matter.

"She's going to get involved again someday," Mark warned. "Be prepared for that. She's going to get on with her life. Don't be jealous of that. You have no *right* to."

Kevin countered with a verbal quick-jab. "You know, Abington, it occurs to me that you're not involved right now, either. Have you or Jennifer ever considered that rather convenient situation?"

"If we had," Mark snarled, stepping directly into the fray, "you should be the last one to care. Stay out of her way, Kevin. Hurt her again and you answer to me—like you should have when you kicked her in the gut and broke off the engagement."

Kevin recovered from that assault and sneered maliciously, an utterly foreign entity compared to the man Mark had known for so long.

"Like I said," Kevin grumbled, climbing into his car, "You and Jen aren't involved." His gaze fastened to Mark's in vindictive accusation. "And when you're thirsty, buddy, you take a drink of water. Right?"


"It's over. Thank the good Lord above, it's over."

Sighing her exhaustion and relief, Jennifer preceded Mark into her apartment. Immediately she peeled off her blazer and hung it over a nearby chair in the living room.

"Don't get me wrong," she continued in a subdued way, "the worst part will be adjusting to the fact that he won't be around anymore. He won't be there for Sunday dinners, or birthdays anymore, or Christmas."

Her breath caught, trapped behind the lump in her throat. She hiccuped on a sob, but Mark noticed her eyes remained unusually dry. Jennifer's tears had been completely spent today, sacrificed in the name of a daughter's love. The visitation was over, so was dinner. Now would be the time for her to gear down and allow herself to re-charge for the funeral tomorrow.

"You were so strong, Face. I couldn't get over it. Your dad would have been proud of you."

Mark stepped up from behind and placed a hand on each of her arms. Gingerly he squeezed, half fearing she'd break she looked so tired and brittle.

But she didn't, and he gave her a silent, unseen nod of admiration. Jennifer possessed an incredible degree of mettle. Perhaps she looked frail right now, but she had done herself and her family great honor in her actions today.

Those words of encouragement escaped him though. As quickly as he thought of them, they vanished, obliterated by the boundaries of what should or shouldn't be said at such a terrible time.

Instead, he stood behind her, allowing Jennifer to lean against him and prop her head against his chest. Seeming restive, she closed her eyes. Mark's gaze happened upon the supple curve of her neck as it tipped back. Her body settled against his, and its curves and textures felt oddly familiar to him now.

His hands moved slowly down the length of her arms and Jennifer felt her tenuous frame of mind go through a change. During the day's services, she had functioned on auto-pilot, mercifully numb. Now, while Mark held her, she felt a reawakening take place. Sensory perceptions came out of hiding, her heart safe in the knowledge that she would be well cared for.

"I can't thank you enough for all you've done for me."

"Thanks aren't necessary, Face." And he meant it.

"But . . ."

"But nothing, Jen. We're friends. Best friends. That simply means we're there for each other. End of discussion. You would have done the same thing for me."

Jennifer's eyes slowly opened, but she didn't lift her head from its comfortable resting place against his chest. "In an instant."

In the middle of the living room, bathed only by the muted gold light of the entryway, Jennifer and Mark stood together. A sudden, powerful onslaught of memory caused Jennifer to blink several times.

"Odd. I can almost smell the pizza and popcorn."

"What?"

"The pizza and popcorn at the concession stands of Chicago Stadium. The Blackhawks hockey game. Remember?"

Mark grinned, finally getting her point. "Our first assignment together."

"My first day at the newspaper, too. We ordered pizza and popcorn and went to the press booth. I could barely speak I was so nervous about working at the *Sentinel*."

Mark laughed at that. "You were a rookie, that's for sure. Tom Brewer had instructed me to babysit, show you the ropes and introduce you around."

"Yep. Remember when, in perfect unison, we sat down, reached for our pizza, then crossed our legs? It was like a precision ballet. I'll never forget the stunned look on your face after it happened.

"I kept expecting *'Twilight Zone'* music to start booming from the overhead speakers." Mark felt the movement of her head against his chest as she nodded. "We laughed so hard the entire press corps wondered what we were up to."

"From that point on . . ." She wasn't quite sure how to polish off that sentence, so it dangled.

Mark understood, and knew precisely what she meant without benefit of elaboration. From that point on they had been inseparable. That insignificant maneuver, that tiny, senseless moment of time—sit, grab a slice of pizza, cross your legs—had bonded them somehow, one of the first things that had broken the ice and connected them, helping to foster the ties that now kept them so close.

"Love ya,' Face," he murmured tenderly.

Cuddled in his arms, Jennifer smiled, feeling that contentment again, the peace of mind that came from having Mark near. She didn't feel in the least awkward about his admission. This wasn't the first time Mark had said as much. He expressed his feelings openly, with a freedom that Jennifer envied. Kevin had crushed that kind of spontaneity in her. Anyhow, actions, she felt, spoke much louder than words. Today had been another shining example of how deep Marks support and caring went.

She stroked his hands, saying in a soft tone, "Right back at you, Mark . . ."

# Three

Stacks of wire copy from the AP and UPI wire services were poised on a corner of Jennifer's desk. So were manila folders and an ink cluttered appointment book. Front and center of this paper work deluge was a pile of phone messages that she began paging through then tossed aside with deliberate carelessness.

Hoping to ward off a headache, she squeezed her temples with gentle pressure from her fingertips, sinking into the swivel chair at her desk.

*Four days off,* she thought bitterly. *I take just four days off to bury my father and chaos ensues.*

"Hey, Jen. You're back kind of sudden, aren't you?"

Jennifer gave Kylie Masterson a fleeting glance. *"Way* too sudden. Look at all this stuff. What happened while I was gone? Massive boycott of the workers? An un-publicized strike? What?"

Kylie sat on the edge of Jennifer's desk, on top of the folders. "None of the above. You're the one who decided to come back, despite everyone telling you not to. That in mind, your co-workers figured massive doses of work would help distract you. Were we on target?"

Smiling, Jennifer stood and gave her friend a tight hug. "Probably. The last thing I want to do is sit around *thinking* right now."

"You held up well at the funeral," Kylie said quietly. "It was a beautiful service. Like I told you then, though, you should take a break and recover a little. You should . . ."

*"Don't."* Jennifer bit off the word with obvious tension, fingering the cowl neckline of her burgundy sweater. Black slacks and flats had been chosen for comfort as well as professionalism. Comfort was of paramount importance to Jennifer now, both physically and emotionally. Her psyche was still extremely tender. "I need work

right now. Sitting around at home will accomplish nothing. I'd only feel worse. Don't push."

"Okay." Cheerfully Kylie swung her legs and gave Jennifer a wicked smile. "Personally I'm delighted you're back. How about lunch?"

"Date."

From that point on, Jennifer wasted no time diving into the work that awaited her. The most immediate situation that needed attention was a dispute brewing between the Chicago White Sox and a player who had been caught at a strip bar after curfew during an away game in Cleveland. Phone calls, to set up interviews and record comments took up a lot of her morning then she turned her attention to writing up sidebars on the story for the afternoon edition of the *Sentinel*.

A short time later, Mark entered the sports department, his progress hampered by an intern who chased after him desperately.

"Mark, the agent won't say a word about contract negotiations to anyone but you." The intern did an imitation of the agent in question. "Mark Abington or nobody. No one else is going to be fair on this issue but him." The intern rolled his eyes. "You got 'em snowed, pal."

Mark couldn't help laughing. The intern referred to a battle for bucks being waged between the White Sox and one of their more note-worthy players.

"I'm on it," Mark replied, unfazed by the circumstances or the compliments. Something else, however, did faze him—stopped him dead in his tracks as a matter of fact. He saw Jennifer at her desk and wanted to throttle her.

*"What's she doing back so soon?"* he wondered. A phone receiver was propped between her shoulder and ear. Scribbling on a pad of paper, she talked and nodded occasionally. She functioned efficiently, with an even-handed temperament, despite the pressure of deadlines that faced her.

Still, the subtle way she kneeded her free shoulder spoke of how worn out she must feel. He was tempted to jump on her case for returning to work so quickly, but he bided his time and held his tongue. For the moment.

In passing, Mark gave her a nod and squeezed her shoulder. Her muscles, he noticed, were knotted tightly. Jennifer winced slightly, and he frowned, but went to his office without comment.

Once again Kevin's rantings after the visitation went on replay through his mind. Jennifer. Romance. The idea, in truth, had never occurred to him before.

After due consideration, he had finally decided to push Kevin's comments aside. Jennifer was attractive, beyond the shadow of a doubt, intelligent, and as sweet as hot butter. But she was like a sister to him. A trusted confidante. Why ruin that, he figured, by becoming lovers? Sex wasn't necessary to gain intimacy between them. They had a kinetic kind of closeness without anything but deep-rooted affection and caring.

Simply put, from the day they had met, they had clicked. He needed nothing more from her. Judging by their two-year history, neither did Jennifer.

Nevertheless, he'd protect her from making a second mistake with Kevin if necessary. Lord help him, he'd punch the chump if Kevin entertained any notion of renewing old ties with Jennifer. Kevin had blind-sided Jennifer without a warning and Mark would be damned if she ever faced that kind of heart break again.

"Jennifer," her desk top intercom crackled, "line two. It's coach Gooden."

Currently processing a story, each click and blip of the cursor sounded like an avalanche exploding around Jennifer's aching head. Taking deep breaths and rolling her shoulders didn't stop the pain of a now full-blown headache so she gave up the effort of evasion and picked up the phone.

"Hello, Coach? . . ."

Mark approached her from behind. Carefully he tried to give her a shoulder massage and she went immediately lax, distracted from her conversation. Not willing to surrender to languor, she swatted his hand away and added a glare for effect. Mark stood aside, patiently waiting for her to end her conversation.

"Hi, Mark," she said after hanging up. "Need something?"

The strain he saw reflected in her eyes pulled hard on his heart. "No, I don't need anything. But you do. Aspirin."

"Excuse me?"

"Aspirin. For your headache."

"Am I that obvious?"

"To me, yes. You okay?" Her stalwart demeanor cracked just a hair, just long enough for him to see the degree of pain she truly felt.

"No, I'm not."

"Then why are you here?"

"I've heard that question a lot today. I'm not a baby. I wish people would trust my judgment. I'd rather be here than anywhere else."

"I trust you, Jen," he assured with haste, but that was a lie. He could tell her nerves were ready to snap. "I only hope you're doing what's best."

"I am."

He didn't feel like competing with the unyielding force of her convictions. "Then I'll lay off. But take it easy on yourself."

She allowed him a slight smile. "Yes, boss. I'm going out to lunch with Kylie. That'll cheer me up."

"Good."

Before Mark left, Jennifer said kindly, "I didn't mean to bite. The massage felt great. Thanks."

He gave her a warm smile. "Anytime, Face."


"Okay, okay! I'm *nuts!* Ignore me and my half-baked ideas. I'm screwy. Forget what I've said if it upsets you so much."

Lunch with Kylie, something Jennifer had looked forward to all morning, was quickly becoming a fiasco.

"Mark has always been a dear friend to me and you know it, Kylie. We've known each other for years and there's never been anything but friendship between us in all that time. You know this, so why are you hassling me about 'romantic chemistry' and all that nonsense?"

"If you don't want me to answer, then don't ask." Arched brow and all, Kylie offered an out-and-out challenge.

"Go ahead and give me your theories," Jennifer said at length. "I promise not to jump at you this time."

"Thank you." Kylie cleared her throat to officially begin her dissertation. "You've gone on and on about how wonderful he was the night your dad passed away."

"Yes. He was. So?"

"If you ask me, he went above and beyond the call of simple friendship, wouldn't you agree?"

Overwrought with a tangle of emotions—pain, greatefulness, exhaustion—Jennifer felt a lump form in her throat. Mark had been a God-send that night, and it seemed Kylie wanted to make it something more.

"Apparently I should have kept my mouth shut about Mark. You're one of my closest friends, Kylie, I thought you knew us well. I thought I could trust you enough to understand he was simply trying to help. I do and I'm comfortable with the situation."

"Then there's today," Kylie continued, being relentless. "He's acting like a protective guardian or something, just like he did at the visitation and the funeral."

"True. He knows what I'm going through. Again, I ask what's the big deal?"

Jennifer's headache was gone, but her stomach felt dangerously close to rebelling against the Caesar salad and Italian bread she had just eaten at *The Bistro,* a deli-style restaurant not far from the *Sentinel.*

"Then what you're saying is that friends can't become lovers."

"Kylie!" Genuinely outraged, Jennifer wanted nothing more than to shove all the comments aside. She didn't want to lose perspective on her relationship with Mark.

Silence filled the space between them and Kylie seemed to realize she had pushed Jennifer to the maximum. "Forget it. I'm a lonely single person whose imagination is running overtime. I don't mean to add pressure or . . ."

"Forgotten." Jennifer said in short. She sipped from a glass of cool, lemon laced iced tea, willing her body to relax nerve by nerve, muscle by muscle.

But she returned to the newspaper feeling uncomfortable with the blunt observations Kylie had made. Discreetly, Jennifer studied Mark while he worked. It didn't seem to her that anything had changed between them.

Until now.

She watched Mark swivel from side to side in his desk chair, a phone squeezed between his ear and shoulder. Unbidden, her thoughts turned to his arms and she watched them now as he jotted down notes and, knowing Mark, added a few comic character doodles to the paper in front of him.

Those arms had held her securely, nestled her beneath a mound of body warmed blankets. He hadn't touched her aside from the arm he had hooked around her waist. He hadn't done anything but tune his body to hers so they would fit together comfortably as they slept.

They had *slept* together. Why, now, did that fact fill her with discomfort—a terrible feeling of awkwardness? Everything between them had been platonic, but the disquiet she suddenly felt couldn't be denied.

Something about Kylie's comments made Jennifer see Mark in a new, more sensual way. Now, considering the night they had spent together, awareness swelled, overpowering the comfort and safety she had always found in being near him.

That first, expectedly awful, week of work passed with speed for Jennifer. She found herself playing catch up to a degree that kept her incredibly busy, but lingering bouts with sadness robbed her of her complete concentration and peace of mind.

Topping it off, at the end of the week Mark called in sick.

"You're what?"

*"Dying,"* he croaked, sounding as though he spoke over a mound of gravel in his throat. "My temperature is 103 and just thinking about food makes me queasy, although an hour ago, I started thinking about a sandwich and some crackers."

"So why are you on the phone with me?" she chided. "You should be in bed, nursing a gallon or so of chicken noodle soup, or hot tea, or . . ."

*"Sunday Sports Feature."*

Her face fell. Of course. He had to write up the Sunday supplement column on the week's top sports story. "You need the files and bios on Ryne Sandberg, don't you?"

"As soon as possible, Face. This article has to be transmitted by tonight. If I don't get the article done, I've had it. What can you do for me, considering I'd owe you big time?"

Jennifer laughed, not needing to be cajoled. Not by Mark. "I can scour your desk for the background information you need and drop them by your place on my lunch hour."

Stuffy nose, rough throat and all, Mark declared, "Consider yourself nominated for sainthood. Are you sure it's okay? I feel bad about you missing lunch on my account."

"Want a deli sandwich?" she asked, ignoring that comment.

"Naw . . ." He paused, seeming to consider his insides before asking tentatively, "Well, maybe a ham sandwich?"

The hope in his voice made her laugh softly, and his coughing jag made her feel even more maternal. "I'll bring soup, too. One of the two should sit well with you. Be there in about an hour."

"You're aces, Jen. Thanks. The Library department sent me a folder the day before yesterday and it's on top of my desk. The official, team bio is in my top desk drawer."

Still smiling, Jennifer hung up the phone and went directly to Mark's office. Since he was organized and methodical to the letter, Jennifer knew she'd have no problem locating the research materials he needed.

Taking a seat behind his desk, Jennifer started rummaging through the neat stacks of paper that layered its top. Almost immediately she uncovered a mounted chunk of gray cement that stopped her hunt for the moment. Front and center of his desk was a piece of what had once been Comiskey Park. Chicago baseball history.

The rock stopped her for a moment, and sadly she stroked the piece. "I don't care what everybody else says, the new park is a replica, but White Sox baseball just isn't the same anymore."

Returning to the task at hand, Jennifer found the packet from the research department and opened the top drawer of Mark's desk to retrieve the player biography he needed. What she saw inside halted her once more.

"Bozo!" she exclaimed with delight.

Extracting a gaudy, red and white plastic ring, Jennifer touched the ridged surface, where Bozo the Clown's face winked at her. Mark had kept it. That realization caused an inordinate wave of pleasure to wash through her.

Not long ago, they had shared a box of Cracker Jack over lunch and they had cut a deal. Mark agreed to let her eat all the peanuts if she would let him keep the toy prize.

Both being Chicago natives, Jennifer and Mark had been delighted to discover the Bozo ring inside, but Jennifer had surrendered her point gracefully when Mark offered to let her keep it anyhow.

"Now to put you to work," she decided aloud, tucking the ring into the pocket of her slacks. Gathering up the background materials, she checked out with Tom Brewer before leaving the offices of the *Sentinel*.

When she arrived at Mark's home, he opened the front door

dressed in a thick, terry cloth robe of deep blue. His red nose and bleary eyes won her immediate sympathy. Unshaven, his hair disheveled, he greeted her with a raspy "hi," and opened the door wider so she could walk inside.

Unable to resist jesting him, Jennifer clutched the files she carried tight to her chest and moved past him with as much distance as possible.

After issuing an "Eeech" of distaste, she relented and gave his forearm an affectionate squeeze. "Lookin' good, Abington."

"Go to he . . ."

"Want this paperwork or not?" She interrupted his nasty proposal with a sweet smile and made a truce offering by handing him the files.

Growling, Mark took the background information and shuffled tiredly toward the living room. "Sit at your own risk. Germs are running rampant around here. I should be quarantined."

"Why do you think I didn't offer you a hug?"

Acting grouchy, Mark mumbled an obscenity beneath his breath, collapsing onto the couch without a second look. Immediately he emersed himself in research materials about Ryne Sandberg. Jennifer reached into her pants pocket and pulled out the Bozo ring. Silently she held it out, just inches from him.

Mark didn't notice until she cleared her throat and asked, "How about this instead of the hug?"

Distracted, Mark looked up. Instantly his face lit with a smile. He took the ring without further ado and even laughed, though the effort cost him a few strangled coughs. "Bozo! My man!"

"I thought he'd make you feel better."

"Yeah, not like a leper as some *other* people have done." Following his pointed look, Mark grinned and put the ring on the tip of his pinky because it wouldn't slide down any further.

Jennifer surveyed Mark's usually spotless living room and stifled a sigh of compassion. Wads of tissue littered the floor. Various newspapers and magazines also decorated the space in front of the couch. Bunched up toward the end of the sofa was an afghan and the end table sported a mug that steamed with hot, fragrant liquid. Probably tea, knowing him.

Jennifer thought of him here, comfortably ensconced beneath the woolen blanket, reading and resting, as he had probably been before she had summoned him to the door. That image worked through her like a ripple, contradictory in that she found it to be incredibly sensual. She could easily imagine herself nurturing him back to health, sifting her fingertips tenderly through his hair, against the roughened skin of his face.

"Think your stomach could handle food yet?" In desperate need of a distraction, she offered up a white wax bag, hoping the aroma from inside would appeal to him.

Mark's brows lifted and he shrugged. "Guess I'll give it a try. My stomach isn't protesting yet."

"I'll warm up the soup and sandwich. Be right back."

When she left, Mark flattened his hand and looked at the kooky clown face that grinned up at him. His shoulders shook with repressed laughter. Bless her heart, but Jennifer could make him feel better, even while he raged with fever.

He sat quietly for a time, thinking of empty Cracker Jack boxes, Jennifer's love of peanuts. *Surprises*. Lord but she was full of them.

When she came back, holding a tray stocked with hot food, Mark gave her a sly grin, a grin that, for Jennifer, brought back memories of the lunch conversation she had shared with Kylie. *Mark Abington. Romance. A damnably unsettling idea.*

Her nerves danced when she looked at him directly, but she went perfectly still otherwise, her throat constricted by feelings she refused to examine in depth. Beware, her mind screamed. For heaven's sake, keep your distance. Don't lose sight of what your relationship with him is all about. *Friendship.*

But her heart refused to listen, countermanding those orders when she leaned close and set the tray across his lap, asking dubiously, "What's on your mind? The look on your face has me extremely suspicious."

"Nothin,' important. Thanks for Bozo, Jen."

Still leaning close, she smiled, utterly lost to her emotions. "Thanks for the peanuts."

# Four

"Karaoke!" Several days later, Kylie tossed an advertisement flyer across her desk, to Jennifer. "Does this sound fun! Read it."

Jennifer gave her friend a tolerant look. "Kylie, your fascination with junk mail from the fax machine absolutely astounds me."

Loftily Kylie answered, "Monitoring our fax mail keeps my finger on the pulse-beat of the city. Now stop griping and read. We should go!"

"Join in," Jennifer read aloud from the sheet, "on the bar craze from Japan that's now sweeping America. Karaoke. Utilizing a laser guided sound system, Karaoke lets anyone sound like a professional singer. Don't know the words to today's top 40 hits? Don't worry—movie screens make you the star and a teleprompter flashes the words of the song you're singing. Live a dream, join in the fun—sing along with Karaoke at the Metro Music Club."

Expectant, Kylie waited. "Well . . . ?"

"Well *what*, Masterson?"

"Let's do it! We could go tomorrow night. Let's get a group together and have a traditional Friday night bash."

The idea struck an appealing chord. Temptation teased. It was time, Jennifer decided, to relax her protective guard and have fun again.

Nearly two weeks had passed since her father's death, but Jennifer's subdued, introverted mood had continued to manifest, and perhaps even intensify. She realized this, but felt powerless to beat the emotional funk that had closed around her.

Confusion about Mark didn't help matters any.

Her work load of late, with upcoming features for the *Sentinel* and research to do, continued to be heavy and she felt grateful for that. She took refuge in her job so she could avoid thinking about him. She found herself wanting distance from Mark, a place to hide so she could think things through and regain perspective on their relationship.

Avoiding an after work gathering, however, would send up red flags for Mark and set them flying. Besides, this was something she wanted to do to give her spirits a boost.

"She's hemming, she's hawing . . . she's deciding . . ."

Jennifer laughed, eyeing her friend. "She's going."

"Great!" Kylie chewed on her lower lip, studying the flyer once more. "I'll find out who else is interested and we'll have a *Sentinel* night on the town."

Not more than an hour later, Mark also accepted Kylie's invitation to the Metro Music Club.

"Count me in." Although he knew he must seem like a conspirator, he went on to ask, "Is Jen going?"

Thinking nothing of his question, Kylie turned back as she left his office. Beyond her, the ever present clamor of the sports department went on at a typical, torrid pace. Computer blips, the scan of wire services, and an occasional shout punctuated the air. Mark loosened his tie and sat behind his paper cluttered desk, waiting for her reply with a lot more anticipation than he showed.

"I'm happy to report she accepted first thing," Kylie answered. "Further, I'm determined to get that girl on stage to sing."

Keying into the computer, he stopped in the middle of calling up an editorial column he was putting together for tomorrow's edition. He gave Kylie a hoot of disbelief. "When pigs fly, Masterson. She'll never do it. She's as shy as they come. Jennifer Meyers is no party animal."

"Ten bucks says she will," she answered shrewdly, defending her friend's honor.

"I'll take that action."

He sounded like a Vegas bookie and Kylie's jaw dropped. "Abington, you're scum."

Laughing, he directed a series of kissing noises her way.

Giggling as well, Kylie retreated in a hurry, calling, "Gross me out!"

\* \* \*

"I'm not a party animal, huh?" Jennifer glowered, thinking, Abington, you just lost ten bucks. "We'll see if he doesn't modify that opinion after tonight."

"I thought I'd let you know before we leave so you could take appropriate action."

"What? Singing or punching him in the eye?"

Standing next to Jennifer in the women's lounge, Kylie leaned over a sink and freshened her make-up. Looking at Jennifer in the mirror, she snickered. "Both, I was hoping. He's so glib sometimes."

"Ain't he just?" Affectionately, Jennifer smiled, touching up her lips with color.

Brushing out her hair, Kylie moaned. "You two are sick."

Jennifer hiked up her purse and gave her hair a final primp with her fingers. "Take my word for it, Mark Abington is in for a surprise."

Kylie hadn't heard a word, but Jennifer had plans. Big plans. About twenty people would be going to the club tonight, so Metro Music would be packed with *Sentinel* employees eager to have a good time. Jennifer planned on being chief among them.

Impatient she prodded, "Are you ready, Kylie? I've got this Madonna tune that just won't leave me alone. I think I'll sing it tonight."

"Like A Virgin?" Kylie asked sweetly, batting her just thickened lashes.

Giving her friend a shove, Jennifer forced her from the restroom and they nearly fell over Mark.

"Ladies, ladies! Settle down. Plenty of time for debauchery, no need to rush . . ." He caught Jennifer's arm in passing. "Need a ride?"

"Nope, but thanks. I'm going with Kylie."

Smooth as silk, breezy and carefree. Perfect. The perfect buddy. Jennifer gave him a smile and walked away, never looking back, not caring to see his reaction.

You've got to cut him loose, Jennifer told herself, and you've got to allow yourself some freedom too. Sadness threatened, but she wouldn't allow the emotion any encroachment. Meyers, she reproached herself firmly, don't consider the consequences. Break away as gently as possible, but keep clear of Mark Abington.

Jennifer began her process of self-awakening as soon as she arrived. About half the large, corner table was full, and she joined right in on the party. Promptly ordering a cocktail, she sat with Kylie on one side and a fellow writer, Jason Hamilton, on the other. Usually she would have sat with Mark, but she didn't allow herself to think about that for long.

"Your reports on the Pan-Am games last week were great, Jason. I never got a chance to tell you that. When did you get back?"

Her message was warmly received. Jason's casual slouch picked up a notch when he looked Jennifer's way. "Two days ago. I got back to the office today and found that my desk has been buried in paper work."

Jennifer laughed easily. "What an ungrateful reception. Did you get your clippings together yet?"

"No, I haven't had a chance to check back issues and make copies of my articles. There just hasn't been time."

Mark stepped up, not speaking as he tuned in to the conversation.

"I can get them for you from the library," Jennifer offered. "That's one less thing for you to deal with. Interested?"

Steady and appreciative, Jason looked at Jennifer anew and gave her a winning smile. "You bet. Thanks, Jen."

"No problem. Happy to do it for you."

"Hey gang." Mark turned a chair around and straddled it. Ordering a beer, he exchanged greetings with his friends.

He had changed from his suit, Jennifer noticed. That's probably why he had been headed to the lavatory at the *Sentinel*. She held her breath, maintaining neutrality as she cast him a quick look. A creme colored polo shirt and black jeans, even in this dim light, emphasized the trim line of his physique, his dark hair and eyes.

Why, all of a sudden, did she feel so tremendously apathetic toward Jason?

Wrong attitude, her mind blared. No, no, no. Enjoy Jason's company. And as though on cue, Jason stood, touching her shoulder. "Want to dance, Jen?"

"You bet."

Don't look back, she cautioned herself. Don't let yourself care. She took comfort in the fact that the song was fast paced rather than slow. Jason was handsome and approachable, but something about him left Jennifer decidedly cold about the thought of garnering his undivided interest.

For an instant her gaze went to Mark, who was deep in conversation with Kylie and Tom Brewer.

*He's just a friend. That's the message he's sending out, so receive it—wide screen. He could care less.*

Well, so be it. Not only would she sing—this so-called "non party animal" intended to dance the night away and socialize with people in the sports department she had unintentionally ignored in favor of Mark's easy, convenient friendship.

She wanted desperately to step into the light for a change rather than live in the safety of Mark's shadow. If she wanted anything more of a man than friendship, she had no choice.

Mark could be gone one day, Jennifer thought, swaying to the beat of the music, smiling into Jason's eyes, eyes she wished were Mark's. After all, not so long ago Mark had come awfully close to leaving Chicago and asking Gwynn Aldridge to marry him.

If Mark made a career move, or began dating seriously, Jennifer would be left without vital spokes of support in her life. She knew she had to allow other people into her life, or she'd end up alone.

The music changed tempo, turning slow and smoky as a jazz-style piece played. Seeming expectant, Jason slid an arm around her waist. "Want to stay out and dance some more?"

Swallowing back her reservations, Jennifer held out her hand and stepped closer. When he laced his fingers through hers, she answered clearly, "Sure."

Unresponsive to the goings on around him, Mark tipped back his beer, swallowing while he watched Jennifer and Jason dance. Bitter, chilly liquid coated his throat. Odd, he thought. She had certainly turned up the charm tonight. And, atypically, she had left him in the dust.

Shifting in his seat, Mark continued to consider the situation. Watching her flirt only confirmed what he felt. Yep, she definitely wasn't acting like the Jennifer Meyers he knew so well.

Not once had she looked at him, or deigned to say more than two words. And why, all of a sudden, was Jennifer seeing stars where Jason Hamilton was concerned? Jason wasn't a bad guy, but Mark felt she could do a damn sight better in forging a new relationship.

Interrupting Mark's revelry, an emcee took to the spacious, curtained stage at the far left of the room. A mini-spot light came alive, illuminating the stage as the dance floor slowly cleared.

"Welcome to Karaoke night at Metro Music!" The emcee's greeting was received with cheers and cat-calls. As he spoke, a movie screen was lowered into place to the rear. "We're going to fire up the Karaoke machine and any one who wants to take a turn singing needs to check in with me. We'll start a list and each group or person will have a chance to perform on stage." He gestured behind him. "On screen, with a live audience. So be brave, sing great, and most of all, have a fun time!"

The man was descended upon immediately. Jennifer returned to her seat and made eye contact with Kylie. They exchanged winks before Kylie stood up and joined the line to sign up for a singing session.

Jason noticed their antics and gave Jennifer a nudge and a grin. "What's up?"

"Nothing at all," she answered coyly.

Kylie returned and whispered, "You and I are fifth in line."

"What are we singing?" When she saw the look on Kylie's face, Jennifer wished she hadn't asked.

*"I've Got a Crush on You.* The Linda Ronstadt version."

"Kylie!"

Acting devilish, she cut Jennifer off. "Your favorite, I believe. So you know the words. It's a gorgeous song, and when I saw it on the line up, I picked it."

"Honestly, a romantic, 1940's ballad? Cut me some slack, Masterson!"

Kylie grinned all the more. "No way, Jen. You wanted to make a statement tonight, so *make a statement."*

Glancing toward Mark, Jennifer found that he studied her as well, his brows furrowed. Their eyes locked and Jennifer knew he hadn't heard the conversation, but he expected her to say something to him, or at least start a conversation. Turning away determinedly, she focused her attention on the stage as the first group of singers took their places.

Mark's features darkened into a full-fledged scowl.


By the time Jennifer went on stage with Kylie, she felt too jittery to notice the encouraging way her colleagues cheered for them.

Once the song started though, Jennifer's doubts did a vanishing act. Sultry, slow, and unbeatably seductive, the music of the Nelson Riddle Orchestra played, sans vocalist, until Kylie and Jennifer started to sing.

The stage lights dimmed and pastel color beamed through the club as a sparkle ball swirled above the stage. Mark watched Jennifer's performance with a smile of respect. Damned if she hadn't proven him wrong.

"It's amazing," he overheard Jason Hamilton say lowly. *"She's amazing."* Mark's gaze swivelled and he saw that Jason spoke with one of the *Sentinel's* chief photographers. "I don't understand why I haven't given her much notice before now." Laughing ruefully, he continued. "I watched her eat some beer nuts a few minutes ago . . . she doesn't just pop them into her mouth like most people. Her tongue kind of darted out and snared it." He sighed. "She doesn't realize how sexy she is. Maybe that's the key."

Mark felt something in the pit of his stomach crumble. Jason nodded toward Jennifer, adding, "It's strange—you work with someone day after day and you can only see them in one certain way. Break the mold and you discover someone entirely different."

The unnamed feeling that had taken a nosedive through Mark's midsection just seconds ago went flying upward, jamming tightly in his throat.

Unbelievable, he thought dazedly. *I'm jealous.*

Try though he might, Mark could find no other way to describe his feelings.

When their turn at the mike was finished, Jennifer made sure she passed Mark's chair. Standing behind him she remarked smugly, "I believe you owe Kylie ten bucks."

That said, Jennifer sat down. Without a word, Mark extracted his wallet from the back pocket of his jeans, yanking out a bill. Never blinking, not looking anywhere else but at Jennifer's face, Mark tossed the money toward Kylie who had just sat down.

"There you go, Masterson." His body was as tight as his tone of voice. "You win."

So, he fumed, Kylie had told Jennifer about the bet. That made Mark angry. He didn't want Jennifer thinking he considered her to be prim, or a stick-in-the-mud. That would hurt her, especially coming from a friend, and he'd no sooner hurt Jennifer than let a White Sox score go unreported.

"Forget it, Mark. Let's split it on a couple of beers." Kylie made the offer, hoping to settle him down.

Mark ignored the peace gesture.

And he didn't get a chance to explain the bet to Jennifer because Jason asked her to dance almost immediately. Watching them leave, the underside of Mark's collar got even hotter. Distance had snaked its way between them like a ribbon of highway. Damn it all. She had been pushing him aside lately and now this bet fiasco. When had their rock-solid friendship turned to quicksand?

Standing slowly, he wove his way around tables and people. His focus centered on Jennifer and stayed put as he crossed the dance floor and interrupted her slow moves with Jason.

Graciously, Jason surrendered his hold on her and Mark stepped forward, curving an arm around Jennifer's waist, bringing her body closely into his.

Why, she wondered sadly, did this feel so *right?* Lord knew it shouldn't. Being held in Mark's arms did nothing to restore her sense of balance about their relationship. The close proximity of his body only muddled matters even more. His touch burned her skin, awakened the needs of her body in a way that sent rhythmic pulses through her body.

"Where have you been tonight, Face?"

Her eyes lifted at the gruff tone he used. "What?"

"Where have you been?"

She acted exasperated. "Mark, what are you getting at?"

"You've been nowhere near me tonight and I'm wondering why. I miss . . ."

Oh, she knew what he missed. The same thing she missed—friendship, light-hearted banter, carefree fun. "Mark, don't pressure me, okay? Grant me a little distance."

*"Distance?* Jennifer, all I've given you lately is distance. What I can't figure out is why you need it. You never have before. Not from me." Gentling his tone, he asked, "What's wrong?"

The last thing she needed right now was his tenderness. It made her ache in a strange, unfamiliar way. "Absolutely nothing, Mark."

His uncouth expletive made Jennifer's ears prickle. She challenged him in a perfectly calm, certain manner. "If you're referring to Jason, may I ask, what do *you* care? Don't you think it's about time I put Kevin and that entire mess behind me? I want to move on. If you perceive my attentions to him as an affront, Mark, I apologize, but I think it's time for me to spread my wings again. Don't you?"

Their dance steps had long since halted. What a terrible, stilted speech for two close friends to share. How could he answer her? His arms were still latched around her waist. Now though, he felt out of place, like an interloper trapped behind enemy lines.

Their eyes were nearly level and Mark stared, trying to figure out what in hell he felt. Had he been that insensitive?

Unknowingly, Jennifer had hit upon his Achilles heel. Of course he wanted her to be happy in a relationship again. But why did he feel so defensive about Jennifer getting involved with another man? That isn't something he could readily discuss with her, though, or reason out.

Mark let shutters close over his emotions. He refused to examine his feelings too closely in the fear that he might actually be jealous.

"Sorry, Jen," he murmured, finally ending their farce of a dance. Garnering his presence of mind, Mark led her back to the table. "You've got a point. I didn't mean to intrude. Come on, I'm sure Jason is waiting for you."

Mark's car keys made a clamor of noise as he threw them aside, hoping they landed somewhere near the hall-table of his foyer.

*She's not being fair,* he railed silently, striding into the kitchen. Tonight's early exit from the Metro Music Club called for a beer that he could ponder over in the comfort of his own home. Twisting the cap off a cold brew, his thunderous disposition failed to improve.

He went to the living room and flopped onto the sofa.

Kicking off his shoes with vehemence, he propped his feet on the coffee table. Mark ignored the plush comfort of well-tanned, leather that cushioned his body, the cooling appeal of the beer he drank. Instead, he found himself recalling the words he had spoken to Kevin Owens following the funeral.

*"She's going to get on with her life. She's going to get involved again. Be prepared for that."*

What shocked Mark is how unprepared *he* was.

"I didn't like it," he muttered aloud, staring gloomily ahead, not seeing a thing. "I didn't like seeing her with Jason Hamilton one bit. I wouldn't have liked seeing her with Kevin either."

Therefore, he couldn't help asking himself—Who would be good enough for Jennifer? Who would meet with his approval?

And why in hell should his approval mean anything?

Disgruntled, Mark clenched his free hand into a tight fist, watching the action with supreme concentration. The degree of frustration he felt was incredible, and at the same time, an anomaly. Mark Abington didn't get frustrated. Frustration wasn't worth the time and effort of raising his blood pressure.

Heretofore, his attitude toward Jennifer had been casual and relaxed, just like everything else in his life. Perhaps he had taken her for granted. Was that a possibility? He simply didn't know anymore, and Jennifer's cool detachment of late hadn't been at all assuring.

So what now? he asked himself.

Simple, he reasoned. Be a friend to Jennifer, like always. Talk with her, that's never been hard to do. Be open with her. And most importantly, don't let her continue this evasion routine.

Don't let the distance become insurmountable.


Despite Jennifer's best efforts, the evening went flat the moment Mark left.

"Meyers, I'd love to play a game of poker with you some time. I guarantee I'd win just by looking at your face. What's wrong?"

Looking at Kylie, Jennifer had cause to recall Mark's words, so similar in tone. *"Everything you are is out there in the open. In your face, Face."*

When Jennifer didn't answer, Kylie continued. "Does your subdued behavior have anything to do with Mark?"

"Yes."

That was all she said, and mercifully Kylie kept her own council about Jennifer's admission, saying only, "If you need an ear, I'm available."

"Thanks." Jennifer shrugged, carefully masking her confusion. "Mark and I seem to have hit a rough spot. That's all there is to it. We'll smooth things over."

"Okay."

Jennifer knew Kylie was humoring her, pretending to believe that simplified, pat answer. Meanwhile, the *Sentinel* bash continued. Jennifer danced with Jason and shared gossip with her friends. Still, Mark wasn't far from her thoughts or her heart.

# Five

"What's this about?" Monday morning, Mark stepped up to Jennifer's desk. Unceremoniously he dropped a stapled sheaf of papers on her desk. Jennifer didn't stop working on her word processor, didn't turn her head.

"What's wrong?" she asked calmly, feigning interest in the story she wrote. She knew what was coming.

"You're not going on the company sponsored trip to Toronto? It's been in the works for close to two months, Jen. How come your name is crossed off the list of people who are going?"

" 'Cause I'm not," came her curt reply, though vulnerability coated her words.

Jennifer gave up trying to concentrate. She stood, consulting a features file that Tom Brewer had assigned her to fact-check. Each Wednesday, the *Sentinel* chose and highlighted an athlete of the week, offering in-depth interviews with local sports heroes and members of non-professional sports teams. Currently, Jennifer was working on a story about a high-school soccer player.

"Why did you change your mind?"

Her shoulders sagged. She didn't look at him when she answered with a bald-faced lie. "I don't feel like it. The trip was in the works for months, like you said. I planned it before my dad died, and now it seems sort of frivolous to me. I'm not in the mood."

Dumfounded, Mark stared for a moment. "Oh. Well, I guess I can understand that—especially after this past weekend at Metro Music." He absorbed her glare without feeling it. "I don't buy it, Jen. You were plenty frivolous just two days ago."

He had a point, and that won him a second glare.

Changing tactics, Mark asked, "What about *'Phantom?'* You already paid for the tickets. You've been looking forward to seeing that show ever since you heard about it. Take it from me, I know first hand. You've been talking non-stop about seeing *The Phantom of the Opera*."

Pressured, Jennifer expelled a stream of air between pursed lips. Count to ten, she told herself. Stay calm. Don't let him get to you or you'll give in and you'll be doomed. "I'll see it here in town sometime."

An angry pause followed that comment. "But the whole point is to escape Chicago for a while, remember? See a different town . . . a different *country?*"

Yes, she remembered. Before, they had joked often about this foreign expedition to Canada. In the midst of studying a page long bio, Jennifer gave Mark a helpless look.

He realized her plight, but couldn't appreciate it. She wasn't the same anymore, and neither was he. But he couldn't quite put a finger on what had infiltrated their relationship and changed it so dramatically. Mark continued to feel like a tide was turning between them and he didn't like that in the least.

So, keeping in mind the promise he had made himself to confront her, he pressed the issue. "Can I be honest?"

"Sure." Warning bells sounded through her psyche. His tone let her know he was going to be just that . . . honest. Why did she dread that kind of openness from him all of a sudden?

"I get the feeling lately that you and I are on egg shells around each other and that's never been the case before. I feel shut-out." He took care not to sound accusing or hurt, just curious, and in need of an explanation. When she didn't answer right away Mark continued, "If it's just my imagination, let me know."

Centering her attention, she asked, "What have I done to make you feel this way? Give me specifics."

Mark didn't flinch away or back track, but one word came to mind. Jason.

He wheeled up a chair from the empty desk next to Jennifer's and sat down. He folded his arms across his mid-section, giving her a look that was equally as direct. "Specifically, I'd say it bothers me that you're giving me the cold shoulder. Lately, we haven't talked, had lunch, or socialized. I know you're still reeling, Jen, but I can help, remember? I'm here for you."

Her thoughts tumbled on a hurricane of emotion. Oh, Mark, I do realize. I do remember. But I'm trying to keep your friendship and not mess it up with delusions about something different—something as risky as love.

Leave me be, she felt like saying, let me sort this out.

Mark watched her face carefully, then continued. "We used to enjoy spending time together outside of work. Fun time." A boyish smile lit his eyes. "You're my spice, Face. I missed you when you decided to hang around Jason." Quickly he added, "It's not just that you were with Jason, it's that you excluded me. Completely."

"I'm not sure how to answer that, Mark," she replied evenly, trying to maintain eye contact with him yet hide her feelings at the same time.

"When we went to the club Friday night, you made it perfectly clear you wanted to be with Jason, but you and I barely spoke. You avoided me. Why? What have I done?"

Silence ensued and Mark straightened, leaning forward on his knees. He took her hands in his. The warm softness of that contact made her body react with a stunning output of pure, sexual heat.

Disturbed, she promptly yanked free of his touch.

"Don't!" she protested, staring at the space where their hands had been. Unable to sort out her feelings, Jennifer couldn't add a word to that by way of defense or explanation.

Mark looked like he had been slapped. "Whether or not Jason Hamilton is a factor in this or not means nothing to me, Jen, but never have you shut me out or pushed me aside." Deliberately his hands dropped, and he made certain she registered the finality of the gesture.

"I won't intrude where I don't belong, but if something's bothering you, let me know. Let's talk about it. Especially if it concerns our relationship. Jason or not, I don't want to lose you."

That said, he stood up and walked away, knowing the next move would have to be hers.


The confrontation about going to Toronto left Jennifer in a stupor. Gone were all the clear cut pathways that had stretched before her just a few short weeks ago. How could she straighten out the tangled mess her emotions had become?

A muddled outlook followed her to the University of Illinois for an interview with the women's basketball coach. From the bleachers of the gymnasium, she watched the squad scrimmage. After practice, the coach joined her and they chatted while Jennifer recorded the comments for an article she was going to write on the team.

The routine procedures of her job kept Jennifer from dwelling on her problems, but she knew without question that Jason Hamilton had to be set straight. She had meant to strike forth on her own, but Jason had gotten caught up in her plans for independence and she wanted to be clear about her feelings toward him before either one of them got hurt.

After all, the only man she could concentrate on, the only one who could stir such passionate reactions within her was Mark. Unfortunately, Jennifer didn't believe his feelings would ever change.

Back at the *Sentinel,* Jennifer set her tape recorder and clip board full of basketball notes aside. She smoothed the fabric of her suede skirt nervously and watched Jason, who sat at a nearby desk.

"Jason," she called, "got a minute?"

He cradled his head, chomping on the end of a pen while he stared intently at his computer screen. Finally he snickered. "Sure. Give me anything but this. My article is going nowhere."

Jennifer gave him an understanding nod of agreement and leaned against his desk. "I've got my own beast to tame with the college basketball profile."

He adjusted his wire rim glasses on his nose and gave her a smile. "I didn't thank you yet for gathering up my clippings. I just filed them away. You helped a lot, and I appreciate it."

"Happy to do it."

Words came to a halt. Jason gave her a questioning look. "What's happening, Jen?"

She tried not to stumble for long, but there was a pause nonetheless while she played diplomat and searched for a way to speak her mind. "I wanted to talk about the other night . . ."

There was a second pause while he nodded and stretched back. "I figured you would. We had a good time."

Something in his words, the tone perhaps, set her at ease. "Yes we did."

"Is that as far as you want it to go?" he asked softly.

She knew, then, that he realized exactly what was on her mind. "It seems like I'm on an emotional rollercoaster lately, not too sure of what I'm after on any level."

"I think that's justified, all things considered."

And she felt sacrilegious, like her father's death was becoming an easy crutch. Self-resentment mounted steadily and she decided that fact would change immediately. "Thanks, but it's not my dad, Jason. It's me."

He took her hand and shrugged in an easy manner. "Don't worry about it, Jen. We both had a good time. Let's leave it at that for now. If other things are meant to happen, they will on their own."

The only thing Jennifer could figure is that fate was dealing her an easier hand than she deserved. "We did have fun, Jason, and you're right. If other things are meant to happen, they will."

But it wasn't Jason she referred to.


"Give me a nosebleed?" Kylie laughed uproariously, giving Jennifer a playful shove as they entered their hotel suite. "The receptionist asks what floor we want our room on and you answer 'Give me a nosebleed?' I love it! You're nuts!"

Chuckling, Jennifer tossed her luggage on the bed closest to the window. "What can I say? I'm a sucker for a view!"

More to prove Mark wrong than anything else, Jennifer had decided to keep her reservation and go to Toronto, a circumstance which delighted her roommate, Kylie.

At Sheraton Town Center, thirty-five stories above ground, Jennifer opened the curtains in front of their window. Overlooking the disk-like structure of city hall, its fountain and park, Jennifer enjoyed the view, watching the bustle of people far below. Flawless sunlight and a rich blue sky made the buildings that towered around them seem to shimmer. A smile of pleasure crossed her face. Two queen sized beds, a comfortable grouping of furniture, and luxurious decor made her feel at home immediately.

"Spectacular, eh?"

Jennifer laughed at Kylie, who stood near the fully stocked bar cabinet, pouring them both a glass of wine. "You sound like a Canadian already, *eh.*"

"Just getting into the spirit of things." She paused, handing Jennifer a goblet and offering a toast. "Let's shop!"

As it turned out, exploring Eaton Center and its layers of boutiques took up most of the afternoon. Despite the fact that this trip was sponsored by the *Sentinel,* the contingent of employees who attended had splintered into small groups and would only touch base as a whole for dinners, and, of course, for the production of *Phantom of the Opera* tomorrow night.

Curiosity prompted Jennifer to ask, "I haven't seen Mark since our flight landed. Is he rooming with Tom Brewer?"

"Who else?" Kylie replied, sounding surprisingly snide.

"What's that tone of voice supposed to mean?"

They walked, side by side, each dressed in silk shorts and blazers. Pausing every once in a while, they admired the sparkle of jewelry store windows and checked on what fashions were up and coming.

"You haven't heard?"

"Heard what? You act awfully put out."

Kylie's wandering came to an abrupt stop and she looked at Jennifer with a stunned expression on her face. "You honestly don't know what's going on, do you?"

"Kylie!"

"Mark's being courted by *Sports Illustrated*. There's an opening on staff for a writer and they're after him to join the magazine in a big way."

*"What?"* Jennifer spoke the word softly, in a deadening, ominous way.

"I figured you knew. He tells you everything. Ever since the magazine started 'flirting' with Mark, Tom's been catering to him like a butler. He knows if Mark goes, there goes an entire slew of readers. *Sports Illustrated* realizes the same thing, so I would imagine they're offering him a whale of a contract."

Jennifer still couldn't believe her ears. "How can you be so sure?"

"Easy. Tom's been chewing up Rolaids like they're candy and he's all but buffing Mark's shoes to keep him on board at the *Sentinel*. He's in a panic."

*Why hadn't Mark told her about the offer?* "How did you find this out Kylie? Did Mark tell you?"

Shaking her head, Kylie pointed toward a window display of haute couture gowns. "No, so I don't think he's made a final decision yet. I only know about the offer because I intercepted three phone calls yesterday between S.I., Mark, and Tom. Apparently the offer is coming down to brass tacks. I knew something big was brewing when the chief editor of S.I. called, so I asked Tom what was going on and he told me about the job offer. He swore me to secrecy, but I figured you already knew from Mark himself."

*"Sports Illustrated* has asked Mark to do articles before. Why didn't you think their calls were simply to have him do another one?"

Kylie gave her friend a benign look. "Think about it, Jen. The chief editor wouldn't call Mark simply to have a chat about upcoming features."

Jennifer's response to that was silence, then a mumbled, "Why didn't he tell me?"

Kylie divided her attention between Jennifer and a dazzling, red taffeta gown. She didn't have a ready answer for that question. "Like I said, I thought he would have told you first thing. That's the only reason I opened my mouth." Pausing, Kylie looked at Jennifer directly. "I'm sorry if I upset you. I didn't mean to."

She shook her head, still reeling from the news. "I feel like throttling him."

*"Jazz,"* Mark offered.

A resounding chorus of nay-saying made the circuit of *Sentinel* employees who were gathered for dinner at the Movenpick restaurant.

"A decent jazz club outside of Chicago?" Tom Brewer chided, "Get serious, Abington. Besides, you get enough jazz at home. Try something new."

"I'm trying opera for the first time tomorrow night. That's enough *new* for one trip."

A round of commiserating laughter followed that statement and Jennifer watched Mark in silence, a now familiar ache swelling in her chest. Desire. Looking at him made needs flow in a warm, heavy pattern through her veins.

Mark was in top form tonight, Jennifer thought, and didn't even realize it. That was the beauty of him. As a reporter, Mark knew the importance of observation and listening, and how important a tool silence can be. He knew better than to monopolize conversations or take advantage of the star status he wore so comfortably.

Yet with friends, he was unguarded and fun, which made him even more charismatic. His charm had the power to captivate. Everyone enjoyed being with him, and the feeling was obviously mutual on Mark's part. Jennifer continued to watch him, her heart, if not her head, utterly seduced.

The arrival of their dinner interrupted Jennifer's train of thought. Although she was hungry, digging into her order of chicken crepes in cream, wild rice, and asparagus with cheese sauce became a means of escape. She didn't talk or joke with the people around her like she normally would have. Introspection ruled her mind, but in its wake she felt only confusion.

Between bites of dinner, Mark kept an eye on Jennifer. He watched her, noticing the way her eyes had darkened, the way she kept ducking conversation. A few times during the meal he tried to catch her eye. Just like she had at the Metro Music Club, though, Jennifer didn't respond to him.

*I've had enough,* Mark thought. *I feel like I don't even know her anymore. This is going to stop.*

He wanted to figure out a way to be alone with Jennifer, but considering how evasive she had been of late, he didn't want to leave her any avenue of escape.

After dinner, Mark moved to the chair across from Jennifer. "In the mood for a walk?"

Shaking her head, Jennifer replied, "Not tonight. I think I might just go back to the hotel and turn in. There's miles of shopping territory Kylie and I haven't covered yet so I'm going to rest up."

"Then I'll see you back to your room," he offered, already standing up.

Panic hit Jennifer like a blast furnace. "Ah . . . no . . . that's okay. We're not far . . ."

He crossed to her chair and helped her slide back, thinking, *You're not slipping off the hook this time, Meyers.* "I happen to be going back to the hotel too. Do you object to me walking with you?"

He phrased the question like a joke, but Jennifer didn't have the inclination to laugh. She caught the undertones of hostility in his voice. Mark took her hand and they said their good-byes then walked out of the restaurant.

Dusk settled over the city, painting purple and royal blue color across the sky. Gusts of cool air refreshed and invigorated Jennifer's senses. Sighing, she closed her eyes. For now she enjoyed the silence that fell between them, glad that Mark didn't pursue the subject of how abrupt she had been at dinner.

Before she knew it though, she found herself talking without really thinking first, speaking from the heart with Mark the way she used to. "I wish I could do what you do to people."

"What's that, Face?"

"You wow 'em."

Mark laughed as though she had cracked the world's funniest joke. *"What?* I wouldn't say I *wowed* anyone, Jen. Don't be ridiculous."

She smirked at his sincere show of modesty. "That's just it, Mark. You don't even know you do it. You're handsome, successful, and you've got a lethal degree of charm. I figured someone better let you in on all this."

Confounded, he pulled on her arm to bring them into full contact with each other. He placed an arm snugly around her shoulders. "Jen, what's gotten into you? Into *us?* For the past few weeks, you've been treating me like a stranger. I can't for the life of me figure out why, but you're uncomfortable with me. Ever since your dad died you've pushed me away with both hands. I realize that his death shook you up, but how come I alienated you? I tried my best to . . ."

Alarmed by the direction of this conversation, Jennifer did her best to put a stop to it. "Never mind, Mark. I'll do better starting now. But you've got to be straight, too."

"When have I not been?"

Armed with Kylie's information, Jennifer prepared to fire. She moved free of his touch and looked into his eyes. "Does the phrase 'Job offer from *Sports Illustrated*' mean anything to you?" Bitterness claimed her voice, making it tremble slightly despite the terse way she spoke. "And if it *does* mean something to you, Marcus Allen, why didn't you tell me about it?"

He looked taken aback. "You didn't hear about it because there hasn't been time. Like I said, you've been avoiding me lately. Besides, I haven't given the idea much thought yet. A firm offer came from the top of the masthead only yesterday." He stopped walking. "How did you find out about it?"

Jennifer hugged her arms tightly across her waist, warding off an inner chill. "Kylie—and don't get mad at her for speaking up. She only told me because she figured I already knew."

"Since we're such good friends and all."

She took no comfort in the snide tone he used. "Don't be a jerk," she admonished.

"Don't be an ice queen," he retorted. "I've had enough of that attitude."

Tension crackled between them, but Jennifer knew how to break it, and avoid the probe of his accusation. A few seconds of silence passed by before she interjected, "You know, if I'm an ice queen, you're a bully."

"A bully?" he questioned, diverted by the audacity of her remark.

"Yeah." The mood between them lightened further when they shared a grin. "You're a bully, and I didn't know that about you before now. Were you one of those awful boys who stole milk money from the other kids in elementary school?"

Laughing, Mark brought her close again, in a light, brotherly way. He made a show of being offended. *"Me?* No. Well . . . not *often."*

Jennifer giggled. "See? You're a *bully."*

They walked through the lobby of the hotel and took an elevator to Jennifer's floor. In front of her door, Mark took the key from her hand and unlocked it for her.

Before she went inside, he stroked her cheek, a single fingertip moving slowly down her jawline and throat. A contented smile crossed his face. Jennifer shivered with need.

"I'm harping on our relationship lately because you mean so much to me, Face. You make me feel good." He took her chin into the cup of his hand. "Seems a pretty simplistic way of putting things, I know, but it's true."

Jennifer held his arms. By now she knew to expect the flood of heat, the tense coil of longing. "I know all this, Mark. Why so sentimental?"

This time he wasn't swayed by her light hearted attitude. "I've got a big decision to make about my life and where it will go over the next five or ten years. Your feelings matter to me, Jen, so don't be shy about letting me know what you think of *Sports Illustrated's* offer."

"I think it stinks," she answered promptly.

"Ahhh, immediate feedback. My appreciation for your input."

"I don't want you to go."

Her voice sounded small. "Why?"

"Because you're one of my best friends and I don't know what I'd do without you. I should keep quiet, though, because that's mighty selfish on my part when you consider you'd be turning down a prestigious job that has a salary and perks to match."

He moved closer. "You never know. That may just be enough for me."

Mark drew her into his arms, tight and true, for a hug that felt as a crackling fire in autumn. Closing her eyes, she laid her head on his shoulder, and soaked in the feelings like a sponge.

After kissing her cheek, Mark pulled away. "Good night, Face."


"Sold!" the auctioneer bellowed. "Your number sir? Thank you, sir. Lot 665, ladies and gentlemen, a paper mache musical box in the shape of a barrel-organ. Attached, the figurine of a monkey in Persian robes playing the cymbals . . ."

A thrill of pleasure gave Jennifer goose bumps. Involuntarily she looked at Mark who sat next to her. They smiled in unison as *The Phantom of the Opera* began.

The Pantages Theatre, a Toronto landmark, hosted the show. With gilt ceilings, elaborate paintings, and newly refurbished, gleaming stairwells, Jennifer thought the Pantages was a perfect place for the *Phantom* to call home. Add to that a glamorous looking crowd and the expectation of a great show, and Jennifer felt like just being at the theatre was an event.

Music and romance wove their spells around her. The close proximity of Mark's body only added to the magic. Sexual awareness blossomed, filling her chest, warming her flesh in slow, inching degrees, like a thermostat.

On stage, the battle between the Phantom and the Vicomte de Chagny was waged with the passion of love. At stake, the heart of the ingenious Christine Daae.

Jennifer felt the emotions of the production as plainly as she saw them enacted on the stage. Watching the play, she felt the length of Mark's arm against hers, the gentle press of his thigh. From time to time, they made eye contact, exchanged a smile or a glance. Each time they communicated in such a way, Jennifer's reactions to him intensified.

Despite the doubts he had expressed last night, Mark seemed to enjoy the performance. During intermission, after a small glass of wine meant to cool and soothe, Jennifer teased him about that fact, saying, "Admit it, you're impressed."

Mark laughed, knowing she was right but unwilling to surrender right away. "Only under duress, Face."

"You were determined to hate opera, but you're having a good time. I can tell."

Doing a quick scan of the people around them, Mark muttered, "Keep it down, would ya'? I've got a reputation to uphold. Opera hater extraordinare. That's me."

Jennifer slipped her arm through his, giving it a squeeze. "Okay, I'll be quiet. Wouldn't want that macho image of yours to be ruined or anything."

"*Strawberries,*" he interrupted, seeming like a light bulb had just gone off in his mind.

"Now there's a fruit."

"Strawberries," Mark repeated, ignoring her antics. "Remember yesterday? At the Movenpick Restaurant? There were tables of strawberry desserts. Let's stop there after the show and get something to eat."

"Sure. I'll bet some after theatre food would go over well with the other guys, too, since they've had to tolerate an evening of opera . . ."

"No—no crowds. Just us, Jen. Does that sound all right to you?"

There was no denying the allure she found in that prospect, but she kept her tone casual. "Sure it does."


*It feels good to be back on even footing with her,* Mark found himself thinking. Matter of fact, he nearly said so aloud but stopped himself. A comment like that might tip the scales all over again.

They shared cappacino and strawberry cheese cake after *Phantom,* and something that had been missing in their relationship lately reasserted itself—unguarded caring. It had been a long time since they had simply laughed at dumb jokes, or spent time alone together without tension sizzling just beneath the surface.

Finally, near two o'clock in the morning, Mark reached for their check so he could pay it. He sighed. "Back to reality tomorrow, Face."

Oddly, she didn't answer him but kept quiet, looking at the tabletop with an unreadable expression on her face.

# Six

"Marcus?"

An uneasy pause coursed the radio airwaves of WCIO. Mark finally replied, sounding doubtful in the extreme. "Yes, Kevin?"

His sports report had just concluded, and Mark braced himself for some off-the-wall comment or observation. Lately Kevin took great pleasure in throwing Mark off kilter during the course of the show.

Snide remarks, cleverly masked by jocularity, had become a favored tool of Kevin's since the funeral. Up until now, his behavior had been annoying, yet easily brushed aside. Something about his tone today though, and his knowing posture, warned Mark of danger ahead. Congenial emotions between them, it seemed, were now passe.

"Clear up a rumor for me, buddy."

"Rumor?" Kevin was acting like he had just picked up on the world's juiciest piece of gossip and couldn't wait to spread the news. Mark's stomach did a slow burn. Kevin, he thought, if you value the sanctity of your health, don't say what I think you're about to say.

"I understand you may be headed to the Big Apple. NYC. Any truth to the word I get that you're going to be taking a job with *Sports Illustrated?*"

"My, my, Kevin. Such an innocent, well-coached question. When did you hear this? And more importantly from whom? After all, my favorite assassin, Guido hasn't had much work lately." Mark took care to keep his tone light-hearted and teasing, but his eyes flashed, boring into Kevin's with venom.

Giving Mark a reveling smirk, Kevin laughed. "No comment, buddy."

"Then I'm afraid my answer is the same. No comment. *Buddy.*"

Gritting his teeth, Mark waited while Kevin sent the program into a commercial. Off air, he thundered, "You son of a bitch!"

Sitting in the obvious cat-bird's seat, Kevin stretched back. He looked as innocent as a lamb. Mark would have been pleased to slaughter him.

"Problem?"

"Many. Since when have we shot from the lip about matters that are of no concern to this station, our listeners, or Chicago sports in general? You're acting..."

Mark stopped himself from launching into a full-blown rage, glancing at the attentive gathering of people in the studio who watched their exchange.

"Obviously you'd like to discuss this, Mark."

Kevin's patronizing attitude snared him like a vice. Given no choice, he followed Kevin to the privacy of the outer hallway and laid into him immediately. "Don't use your show to stomp on me. I'm getting sick of it! I'm the sports director here for one reason alone—you and I wanted to work together. We've been friends since college. That is—we used to be friends. Why are you on my case? Thanks to your indiscreet comments just now, the media is going to be all over my back wondering what in hell is going on!"

Refusing to repent, Kevin clucked his tongue, the gesture intentionally condescending. "Price of your success, buddy. Besides, that gigantic ego of yours needs some taming, Abington. Don't start thinking you're above the crowd because of this offer you've got going from S.I."

That accusation rolled right off Mark, for he knew the statement didn't ring with an ounce of truth. He also knew exactly why Kevin was acting so hostile—and it had nothing to do with ego, or professional status.

"Oh. I see. Then Jen doesn't enter into the picture at all? She's not the reason why you're acting like such an ass?"

"Why should she? I have Brenda."

Now it was Mark's turn to smirk. "You may have Brenda, *pal,* but Brenda doesn't have *you.* She never has. I think you're getting bored with her and you're taking another look at Jennifer. Well forget about it."

Dumbstruck, Kevin gaped. Mark knew he had scored a bullseye, so he pressed his advantage. "I said it before, but I'll say it again—

Jen and I are friends. *However,* don't even *think* about seeing her again, Kevin. I won't allow it to happen."

Threatening, Kevin moved closer. "You won't allow? Well hear this, Abington, you may not have a choice in the matter."

Unperturbed, Mark stood his ground. "Keep away from her, Kevin. After the stunt you pulled by dallying with your producer, I'd say Jennifer deserves better."

"Don't give me your self-righteous attitude, Abington. Let Jennifer be the one to decide."

"Fine." Mark surrendered the battle with a negligent shrug. "I *will* leave it to Jen. She's too smart to make the same mistake twice."

For a moment, looking into Kevin's embittered face, Mark regretted taking up the noble stand of being a pacifist. Forcing himself to settle down and ice his temper, Mark dug his hands into the pockets of his pants. Further he warned, "If you put me in a situation like this again, or embarrass me once more on the air, I'm out of here. I'll quit. Let's see how station management takes that."

It was turning into a terrible Monday morning. Mark lamented that fact as he left the studios of WCIO and drove to the *Sentinel*. He wasn't surprised to discover phone messages on his desk from several of the competing newspapers and television stations of Chicago.

None of the pink slips offered an indication of what these people wanted, but Mark knew the media hounds were after him for details about the job offer and the answer to one question alone—Would he be leaving?

In the quiet of his empty office, Mark did an uncomplimentary impersonation of a reporter. "What kind of a job offer is it? What kind of package could send one of Chicago's lead sports columnists packing for New York City?" Growling fiercely, he cursed, "Damn you, Kevin."

Not long after Mark's arrival, Tom Brewer joined him in his office. "I hear you've been swamped by information seekers. I listened to the program this morning and I've been waiting for you to show up ever since. How do you want to handle the situation?"

Seeing the concern on Tom's face and the weary way he carried himself made Mark feel like he should apologize. Granted, he had no control over what people would say about the job offer from *Sports Illustrated*. Nevertheless, Tom's attitude made Mark feel bad.

The thought of his boss being so concerned didn't sit well on his shoulders.

"I haven't made a decision yet," he hastened to inform. "What ever you think would work best is fine by me."

And it turned out to be Tom who offered comfort. "I understand what you're going through, trying to make such an important decision about your life, but I feel like there's nothing I can do. I can't be an impartial listener, or offer you an unbiased opinion. I want you to stay right here. But I don't want other people—especially these media hounds—pushing you to make a choice before you're ready."

Coming from a chief-editor, that was an impressive endorsement. It made Mark feel even worse. He realized of late how difficult it would be to leave the life he had built in Chicago.

"Then I won't return the phone calls. If they call again, the company line can be that I have no comment about the offer at this time. Hell, it's the truth."

Tom stood and clapped a hand against Mark's back. "That's what I was hoping you'd say. Thanks, Mark." He was about to leave, but he turned back. "I've worked as an editor for newspapers all over the country, but I've never come across a sports writer with as much reader appeal as you have." Encompassing the messages with a hand gesture, he ended, "Once the news broke, I guess I should have expected this."

Jennifer happened into Mark's office a short time later, just as he was setting a fresh cup of coffee on the corner of his desk. Slouched down in his chair, Mark looked rueful as he paged through the now rumpled set of messages—one by one.

"Mark, do you have your notes from the press conference ready for . . ." Looking at the taut lines of his face, his bleak expression, caused Jennifer to do a quick shift of gears and forget about work for the moment. She walked to his side of the desk. "What's wrong?"

Handing her the slips of paper, Mark shook his head. "Take a look."

"The *Trib*, the *Sun-Times*, WLS, WBBM." Her eyes lifted to meet his. "What's this about? Why do these people want to talk to you?"

"I can tell you true, Face, they're not after the final score from last night's Cubbie's game. Obviously you didn't tune in to Kevin's program this morning."

"Not today. I usually do, but I had an early interview set up so I didn't get the chance. Why? What happened?"

"He announced that I might be going to New York."

Then it dawned on her. Of course. News of the job offer had been leaked to the media, deliberately, by *Sports Illustrated*. Kevin had obviously been first to hear of the offer and had jumped on the information like a vulture, ready and willing to start a fire storm.

But why? Why would he put Mark in the position of having to fend off the press and face such pressure about his professional life? They were *friends*.

"Aaahhh, the squeeze and tease technique," she observed, feeling sorry for Mark. Like it or not, he was being put in a touchy situation. "S.I. puts the pressure on for a decision by tantalizing your competition with the hope that you'll soon be history."

"You've got it, Face. Soon each one of these stations and papers will gleefully report that I'm being courted by S.I., and very well may leave Chicago. They let the public know what a great offer I've got going and consequently my readers will start thinking about getting their sports information elsewhere. After all, they figure, I'll soon be in New York. How could I possibly turn down *Sports Illustrated?*"

That was her concern exactly. "They're trying to make the decision for you. That's a very effective play—for everyone but you. What I don't understand is Kevin. He didn't need to make this public knowledge. That's a rotten thing to do to a friend."

*"Friend?"* Mark muttered. But he quickly continued, not wanting to talk about Kevin with Jennifer. Yet. "This does tell me how serious *Sports Illustrated* is about their offer. They want me on board badly. They leaked, wanting to step up the pressure on me to make a fast decision, and Kevin was obviously listening."

Jennifer leaned against the top of Mark's desk, holding a file folder against her chest. "Why? And while we're at it, why is he on your hide so much lately? He's really been pushing the limits with you during his show."

Mark stared into her eyes long and hard, wondering how much to say, and how soon. For now, there simply wasn't enough time to explain Kevin's behavior. "Later, Face. I'll explain about Kevin later. Suffice to say we've had a major falling out."

If caring could be felt in a silence, Jennifer thought, this was one such moment. Ignoring the situation with Kevin, she asked softly,

"What about the offer, Mark? Are you as serious as S.I.? That's what matters to me the most."

Tossing the papers aside, Mark gave her a bewitching smile. Jennifer felt her stomach swirl at the look on his face.

"You've always been my biggest and best supporter, Jen. I haven't thanked you for that lately. You ask a good question. Trouble is, I'm not sure how to answer it." He shook his head. "I sure as hell don't need this kind of garbage. Now everybody is going to want details. Am I going? Am I staying? How much money? What are the fringe benefits? You know me, Face, I'm a sports lover who happens to write pretty well."

A modest statement, she felt, if ever there was one. Silent, she let him continue.

"I enjoy the people I meet, so I socialize a lot—that makes me high profile. But I'm not into the money game, or prestige for the sake of prestige."

"And you have both money and prestige right here, Mark."

She wanted to take the words back, though, as soon as she said them. The last thing he needed was more opinion, more pushing, and here she was, practically asking him to stay on at the *Sentinel*.

"Oh, Mark, I'm sorry. I should learn to keep quiet sometimes." Contrite, feeling as though she had been a little too open for her own good, Jennifer moved to make a rather hasty exit. "I almost forgot what I came in for. Get me the notes on Phil Jackson's press conference when you get a chance, okay?"

He watched her walk away and return to her desk. In actuality, Mark wanted to talk with Jennifer. She would make a terrific sounding board for some of his thoughts about the job offer, and he wanted to cue her in on the real reason behind Kevin's hostility. But now was not the time.

At the *Sentinel* late the next day, Mark rounded a corner, walking through the doorway of his office. Absorbed by the memo he read, he walked behind his desk and was prepared to sit before he noticed something amiss . . .

He happened to be looking downward, so the first thing he saw were a pair of cream colored, suede pumps. Long, slender legs. Perfectly sheer cream hose. Lifting his head slowly from the paper, he detected the linen fabric of a skirt and a hemline that had been arranged neatly above a woman's knee.

He looked no further than that, but chuckled lowly. Additional identification would be unnecessary. He'd know those legs anywhere.

Without looking up, he greeted, "Good afternoon, Gwynn."

He sat down, casual and nonplussed, which caused Gwynn Aldridge to laugh. "Good afternoon," she retaliated with equanimity. "Knucklehead."

Mark tossed the paper aside, finally looking up with a broad smile. Oh, yeah. It was Gwynn alright, straight off the five o'clock news and the boutiques of Fifth Avenue in New York City.

Knowing her as well as he did, Mark harbored absolutely no illusions about why she had suddenly shown up in Chicago.

He stretched back a mite and steepled his fingers, studying Gwynn intently. His eyes took survey of changes she had gone through, the subtle differences caused by time and distance. It had been a year, after all, since they had been lovers—a successful, glamorous couple on their way to happily ever after.

Content to be perused, Gwynn lifted a perfectly shaped brow and awaited his observations.

Physically she was much as he remembered, with unbound, thick raven hair, the clearly defined structure of a beautiful face, inquisitive, lively eyes of light brown.

There were differences, though, between this new reality and the memories he possessed. Gwynn Aldridge, at a single glance, personified success and sex appeal. Elegance, too. Heavy doses of that. Mark felt delight at seeing her again, but was decidedly cold otherwise. That surprised him.

Meanwhile, Gwynn kept right on watching him.

Finally, he decided to give her the opening she needed to express why she had gotten homesick for Chicago all of a sudden.

Slyly, he observed, "Sweetheart, you shriek Manhattan."

He stood and crossed to the chair next to hers, offering both his hands. She took them promptly as he sat down. "Did you expect any less?" Then she jumped right to it. "And, *sweetheart,* from what I hear, you may soon suffer from the same malady."

*"Really?"* Mark pretended that was the biggest piece of news he had heard in years. They released hands and Gwynn finally gave up her playful pretense and glared at him.

"Yes, Knucklehead. *Really.*" Manhattan vanished in a blink and found itself replaced by the real Gwynn. The one Mark had cared for so deeply a year ago. Her eyes shone with an appealing degree of enthusiasm and her posture lost all semblance of cool and restraint. "I know about *Sports Illustrated*. Found out from a friend of a friend that they're not only offering you a job—they're offering you the sun and the moon to join staff."

Mark smirked inwardly at the way she eagerly stressed her words. But the smile remained. He had always enjoyed one-upping Gwynn because she could, most times, one-up him right back.

"A friend of a friend?" he asked sarcastically.

Gwynn settled back into her chair, looking overly bored. "Of course, Mark. The media in New York, as you know, is a tight knit bunch. We monitor each other closely. They spot a blemish on my nose while I'm anchoring the news and reporters from *Newsday* want to do a feature on it. So what gives? When do you leave? Why didn't you tell me about it? This is great news!"

Mark had burst out laughing after her inane comment about blemishes. His enjoyment only increased at her belief that he was already packed and set to go.

"Gwynn, my acceptance of the job offer isn't a foregone conclusion. Not by a long shot."

Had he told her he was joining a commune in outer Mongolia, Mark couldn't have shocked her more. Her coral kissed lips formed an "oh" of surprise and she was silent, but her expression said it all—disappointment.

Mark stood with a groan and went back to his desk. "It's not as simple as you think . . ."

The phone on his desk started to buzz. Mark felt tempted to forget the cursed thing, but couldn't. Ingrained habit refused him peace until he answered the call.

Gwynn scowled as he lifted the receiver, saying quickly, "I won't let you avoid this topic, Knucklehead."

Unfazed, Mark picked up the receiver. "Hello? Oh . . . yeah, Face. I'll find it in a minute. I have a visitor right now . . . one you'll want to see. Got a minute?" He looked up with a rakish, killer grin, hoping to charm Gwynn onto another subject, and discovered she was watching him with a curious expression on her face. "Okay, stop by my office as soon as you can."

Mark hung up and Gwynn asked, "Jennifer still works here?"

"Yeah. How'd you know . . . ?"

Gwynn smiled, a small, nostalgic curve of the lips. "She's the only one you'd ever call Face. Remember our double dates with her and Kevin?" Before Mark could answer, or fill Gwynn in, she continued. "I never got an invitation to their wedding. I wouldn't have been able to come, being in New York and all, but I would have liked to get them a gift."

Mark moved quickly to set Gwynn straight. "They didn't get married."

A second look of shock. "Really?"

There was an uncomfortable pause as Mark contemplated the most sensitive way of explaining what had happened. "Kevin met another woman and Jennifer ended up getting badly hurt."

There was a look of pure outrage on Gwynn's face. "What a jerk!"

"I couldn't agree more," he said ruefully. "Kevin and I haven't been on steady ground lately."

"Mark! That's terrible. What's been going on since I left? The city's gone to pot."

"Times have changed."

"And not for the better. Poor Jen. I hate the thought of her being drop kicked like that. Is she okay?"

"Yes. She's well rid of him I say, although she hasn't been involved since. It's been a rough year for her. She lost her dad just over a month ago." Then, to escape talking of maudlin things, Mark forced a cheerful note into his voice. "We've muddled through, though. She'll love seeing you again, Gwynn."

Something had started clicking in Gwynn's mind. He could see that plainly in the shadows that swept across her face then vanished as quickly as wisps of fog.

Her face brightened. "It'll be good to see her again."


Not much later, Jennifer knocked on the door to Mark's office. She was summoned inside, and his voice was resonant with laughter. She stalled on the spot when she walked inside and saw who his "visitor" was.

"Gwynn. Hello."

Gwynn approached her with an affectionate smile. "Hi, Jen."

Following a brief hug, Jennifer looked at the woman, pushing back her feelings with as much strength as possible. But one inescapable thought got through. Loud and clear. *What in hell was Gwynn Aldridge doing in Chicago?*

Truthfully, though, she already knew. Gwynn wanted to do whatever she could to get Mark to go to New York.

Fury claimed her heart, but that emotion was masked by the face of surprise she wore. "It's good to see you. When did you get into town?"

"A few hours ago. I haven't even checked in to my hotel yet because I wanted to see Mark first."

I'll just bet, Jennifer thought, riled by what she saw as an obvious, inexcusable form of manipulation. Damn Gwynn anyhow. Now Jennifer felt like she had truly lost him. As if Kevin and the rest of the media junkies weren't bad enough about applying pressure, Gwynn had sashayed into town to pull a few strings of her own.

The *Sentinel* didn't seem to stand a prayer of keeping Mark on staff now.

Turning, Gwynn did a graceful cover for the awkward silence that had befallen Mark's office. "Dinner tonight, Mark, at your place, like you promised." She joined him behind his desk and placed a leisurely kiss on his cheek. "I'll make pork chops if you'd like."

Before leaving, she took Jennifer's arm. "I'll be in town for a few days. I've missed you, Jen. We should have lunch, and catch up on things. Does that sound alright to you?"

Looking steadily into Gwynn's unassuming face, Jennifer felt her heart freeze over. In her mind, she was already starting to say her farewells to Mark. "Sure, Gwynn. That would be fine."

Jennifer saw something akin to victory flicker through Gwynn's eyes, but Gwynn simply nodded with a smile and gave Mark a long, last look before leaving.

Jennifer was completely out of breath. Her heart thundered beneath the sweater she wore. Pain squeezed against her, making her feel oddly light headed.

She stared at the closed door, unmindful of Mark, of how strange she must appear. Feeling a gentle touch on her shoulder, Jennifer started. Looking at Mark she wanted so badly to just go limp, rest her head on his chest, beg him not to leave, not to give in to Gwynn's obvious charms . . .

"Face," he asked, his tone as soft as satin, "do you want to talk about this?"

Jennifer turned away quickly, shaking her head. "No, I'm fine. Stunned, but fine."

Mark wasn't satisfied with that answer. He gripped her upper forearm and refused to let her leave. "You look a little pale to me. If it's Gwynn that bugs you, let's . . ."

Jennifer couldn't help herself. Words started spilling out before she could consider them, or stop the flow. In an angry, tightly controlled voice, she said, "Don't let her get to you, Mark. If she's who you want to be with, that's one thing. But you let her go when she left for New York and neither one of you have looked back—at least not that you've told me about. She's here for one reason only—to nudge you ever so gently toward leaving Chicago and joining her in New York.

"Well I demand equal time. I'm going to get my two cents worth in before she does. Forgive me for saying this, Mark, but I don't feel like shopping for a bon voyage gift. I don't want you to leave."

Before he could reply, or keep her in place, Jennifer stormed out of his office.

She didn't stop walking. Jennifer checked out for the night and left the newspaper immediately. Regret pounded her spirit as effectively as a pro boxer.

She regretted being so bare-faced honest, regretted being so manipulative in her own right, and most of all she regretted feeling so damned heartsick at the prospect of losing Mark Abington to Gwynn Aldridge.

There was no mistaking her feelings now. Layered just centimeters beneath the rage she felt was love and jealousy, tangled so tightly together they were indiscernible from each other.

Powerless to fight any longer, Jennifer let her feelings wash through her, experienced each one with draining force. The name Gwynn Aldridge slid down the length of her spine like cold slush. A gourmet dinner at Mark's place. Come hither looks. Success painted over every fiber of her being. Yes, Gwynn Aldridge was back in town all right.

She kept up her pace and turned onto Wabash Avenue, starting to breathe hard as she put more and more distance between herself and the gray stone building that housed the *Sentinel*.

The pain she felt was unbelievable. Needs like this knew no respite, no peace. Long ago, the ground work had been laid between herself and Mark, the rules plainly established. Friendship. Trust. Uncomplicated companionship. *That's all.*

*But that's not enough.*

Crisp air was stirred by a strong, lakeshore wind. Jennifer's hair whipped in front of her face. She missed her spring coat, despite the sweater she wore. She fought off the wind by hugging her arms tightly against her body.

People jostled past. The smell of exhaust fumes permeated the air. Car horns added impatient sound to the life of the city as Jennifer neared her apartment. She needed movement, needed to expend the energy she felt, and had turned utterly oblivious to everything but a sense of futility.

She loved him. She loved Mark Abington completely and overwhelmingly.

But it was too late now. Why had it taken her so long? Why had she made this discovery when it was too late to do anything to change their relationship? The man she could be happy with for a lifetime had been her best friend for years—and soon he would be gone.

The situation went steadily downward.

Early the next morning, Jennifer received a phone call from Gwynn, who sounded extremely chipper. "I hope you were serious about accepting a lunch invitation, Jen. I'd like to see you. Today, if possible."

Jennifer winced and silently counted to ten while she formulated a reply, or, hopefully, a reason to say no. Unfortunately, she couldn't wrangle her way out of this one. "Sure. What time?"

Gwynn gave an appealing, sincere laugh. "You tell me, Jen. You're the one who's working today, not me. When would be good?"

Never . . . "One o'clock would be fine."

"The Bistro is still a favorite haunt, isn't it?"

Damn. She was even being thoughtful. "You bet."

"Great. We'll meet there."

Jennifer hung up the receiver in slow motion, wishing she could go numb from the heart on down. She didn't want to face Gwynn, or Mark, for that matter, but he hadn't been in yet this morning.

She felt torn. One moment she wished she could just see his face, or reach out to him. The next second she hated feeling that kind of desperate longing.

## Seven

"I was sorry to hear about Kevin. I think it's cruddy what he did to you."

"I'm getting over it, Gwynn, but thanks for the loyalty."

Jennifer spoke, but kept her focus on the Reuben sandwich she ate, unable to look her luncheon companion directly in the eye. They were still in the process of pleasantries, but the topics were gradually circling inward, toward more personal, private places. Consequently, Jennifer felt her guard rise up like a drawbridge.

"Mark and I were talking about it last night," Gwynn continued. "He says he feels guilty that you got hurt."

That comment brought Jennifer's attention to the fore in a hurry. "What?"

Gwynn placed her fork on her plate and ignored her shrimp salad. "Mark is as protective of you as ever, Jen. I'm glad, with all that's changed since I left, that the two of you have stayed so close. The feelings you share run deep."

Jennifer ignored that accolade. "He feels bad about Kevin? That's the first I've heard it."

"He introduced the two of you. He even nurtured the relationship, hoping the two of you would be happy together." Gwynn shook her head. "He cares about you a lot."

The words were kind, but they sent Jennifer's stomach plummeting. Typical of Mark, to watch over those he cared for. More than anything else, Gwynn's words convinced her that friendship is all she would ever get with Mark, and friendship is what she would have to be content with.

"I wasn't aware of his feelings."

Jennifer wanted to let the topic drop there, but Gwynn had other plans. "My point is you're very important to Mark. He counts on your input, cares a lot about your feelings."

Jennifer held her breath and looked straight into Gwynn's eyes, feeling hostility broach the cold brick wall that had closed in around her.

"So . . . ?"

Gwynn folded her hands and viewed Jennifer intently. "You care about him. You two are close." With more emphasis, she added, "You want to see him do what's best, I'm sure."

Steeling her back, Jennifer answered forcefully, "Yes I do. What are you getting at?"

"Jennifer . . ." Gwynn paused and searched for the exact way to express her view. "Jen, the best place for Mark to be right now would either be Los Angeles or New York." She waited there, watching closely for reactions. Jennifer gave nothing away. Continuing with a tad more uncertainty, Gwynn kept her tone deliberate and purposeful. "He's near the top of his field, but he's not the creme of the crop. For that, he's got to achieve . . ."

"Achieve what, Gwynn?" She couldn't keep the starch from her voice. "And for whom?"

"Jennifer, I don't like that implication at all. I'm simply saying he belongs in New York City. The exposure he'll get, the benefits to his career, can't be attained elsewhere. I think you know that as well as I do."

"I know no such thing. Mark is doing just fine right where he is. After all, Gwynn, Chicago is hardly provincial."

Her mouth twisted wryly. "Compared to New York it is."

Jennifer would have loved to fight that age-old battle with her—Windy City compared to Big Apple—but frankly she didn't feel like expending the energy. Not in the mood she was in. Not with Gwynn Aldridge.

"Where do I fit in? What is it you want from me?" Pleased to detect the slight flinch Gwynn made, Jennifer waited patiently for a reply.

"I want nothing from you, but you're very close to Mark, like I've already said . . ."

"So?"

"I want you to encourage him to do what's best, Jen. It's plain to see that New York is where he belongs now. He can go no further in Chicago. As a writer, he's the best of the best. He needs to be convinced that the move to *Sports Illustrated* will serve him well in the long run. You could do that. He'd listen to you. Mark will stymie here, Jen. Is that what you want?"

"What I want is immaterial. What *Mark* wants is paramount."

"But . . ."

Jennifer cut off her rebuttal. "There are no buts on this issue, Gwynn. If you expect me to pressure him to leave, forget it. If Mark wants to go to S.I., that's his choice to make, not mine. *Not yours.*"

The meal had been long since ignored. Gwynn sat back in her chair, staring at Jennifer. "You're a big part of what's holding him back, Jennifer, and that's a shame. I think if he got any encouragement from you, he'd take a chance and go to New York. He's extremely talented, but he needs more exposure. You're looking at this situation like I'm pushing him to New York for my own gains. I'm not. Actually, I have the feeling you may do more to keep him or send him off than anyone else. Please believe that I'm only trying to . . ."

"I don't buy in to any of this, Gwynn," Jennifer cut in. "I can't, considering that you and Mark were so deeply involved before you left Chicago." Speaking those words aloud tore at the fabric of her heart. The thought of Mark cradling Gwynn in his arms, loving her, eroded Jennifer's inner composure.

"True, Jen, but I don't think Mark and I will be able to pick up our relationship where we left it a year ago, if that's what you're implying. Times change."

Gwynn had no idea how true that was. Jennifer couldn't resist asking, "What makes you say that?"

"Dinner was . . . different. We enjoyed being together, and we spent hours getting caught up . . ." Gwynn shrugged elaborately. "I can't quite describe it, Jen, but where I expected warmth he seemed withdrawn from me. Remote. He didn't speak of another woman, but I could swear he felt uncomfortable with me."

That didn't sound at all like Mark. "Did you discuss the job offer with him? Maybe he felt uneasy about that."

"Only in general terms." Negligently she waved her hand. "I wasn't as direct with him as I've been with you."

Pressing her hands together tightly, Jennifer warded off a chill feeling that she was being manipulated by a master. This woman knew exactly what she wanted and fully intended to go after it.

Gwynn planned to use her as an "ace in the hole," hoping to stoke Mark's ambition to move ahead in his career.

Nearly an hour had passed and Jennifer would be expected back at the paper soon. Resentment would have overridden all else if she hadn't felt the threat of impending loss so acutely. Strange, but she missed Mark already. Sands were shifting rapidly around her feet, sucking up feelings, people, and times she would never be able to experience again.

*Times change . . .*

They left the Bistro, but Jennifer returned to the *Sentinel* on her own. She felt an awful reluctance to meet up with Mark, to talk with him, or try to hash things out. Openness now would be incredibly dangerous.


Dinner with Gwynn the night before had been an unqualified disaster. Mark entered the lobby of *Sentinel* headquarters, tracing a route to the elevators on automatic. He ignored everything, the chime of floor stops, the chatter of people who crowded around him. On the fifth floor, Mark maneuvered his way out, his features darkened by an intense scowl.

He had sped back to the paper following an interview with this week's "Athlete of the Week." He had forsaken lunch, knowing he had no appetite for food at the moment.

Why had an evening in Gwynn's company left him feeling so cold? The chemistry that had been so rich between them just a year ago had evaporated.

He couldn't figure out why.

And, since he was considering puzzling circumstances, what in hell had gotten into Jennifer yesterday? Her blow up had left him shaken.

As he walked toward his office, Mark saw her, at work on the computer. He didn't miss a beat but went directly to her and knelt at her side.

Jennifer spared him a glance of question, nothing more, until she asked softly, "Did the pork chops taste good?"

"Rotten." Taking hold of the arms of her chair, Mark turned her to face him. He felt his hackles rise when Jennifer crossed her arms against her chest. Her insolence made him hit below the belt. "It would help to have a friend to talk to, but you've been nowhere to be found."

No nicknames, no tenderness. And the message got through to Jennifer clearly. Guilty, she looked down, then up. "I'm sorry."

"You gave me your opinions then you vanished. I never got a chance to . . ." Oddly he found he couldn't express what he felt, couldn't find the words to say how it had hurt to not have her nearby, ready to lend an ear, a shoulder, friendship. "I . . . I wanted to talk, Jen." Tenderly he took one of her hands and held it firm. "I spent last night with Gwynn, being pushed into a corner about this damned job offer, and all I kept thinking was how I wished I were with you, really talking, saying how I truly felt, without pressure or judgment."

He couldn't have won back her good graces any faster. The steel resolve crumbled. Jennifer's hostility drained, as did the uncertainty and doubts. Mark had a knack for making everything in her world settle on its rightful foundation.

"I felt out of place, Mark." Her throat tightened, turning her words husky. "I didn't want to barge in where I don't belong. Gwynn wanted to have a . . . quiet . . . dinner with you. What did you expect of me? I knew she'd pressure you, so, I pressured you first because I'm afraid of losing you. I stormed off because I knew I was wrong, but I won't take the words back, or the way I feel. To do that would make me a hypocrite. So, I figured I'd give you space so you could sort things out on your own."

"Come here, Face." He pulled her up and led the way to his office, closing the door behind them. Immediately he began to speak. "There is no place in my life that you don't belong. The fact that you felt uncomfortable with me . . . God, Jen, *don't*. Not ever. Not after all we've shared. You're . . ."

She held her breath and waited, prayed, hoped . . . "I'm what, Mark?"

His eyes bore into hers. "Jen, there are all kinds of flowery phrases I could use to describe what you are to me, but words would make it trivial somehow. Our feelings are a given. That's what hurt the most yesterday—I wanted so badly to turn to you, and find a harbor in the storm, only to find you had disappeared. I needed you."

The fact that she had let him down, especially after everything he had done for her, was crushing. Tears stung. She refused them. Emotions swelled. She welcomed each and every one—even the regret she felt at not being there for him. She'd make it up to Mark now.

"Needed—as in the past tense?" she asked hesitantly.

"Need *period*. End of discussion."

Jennifer smiled at the elaboration, wondering if all the love she felt on the inside could be seen on the outside. She finally sat down and Mark followed suit.

"Talk to me," she invited. "What happened last night?"

Mark explained. Gwynn hadn't been at all subtle about the job offer. Apparently she didn't feel a trace of shame at her brazen tactics. Only one thing mattered—making him see the light of day and accept the position with *Sports Illustrated*. Gwynn had left no question that she wanted Mark to make fast tracks to New York. To her. She had been equally as blunt on that count.

Gwynn had always been ambitious, and possessed a clear knowledge of what she wanted out of life. Therefore, the pressure she applied hadn't surprised him too much. But she had been stubborn, too, and that's something Mark would not abide by.

"I don't want anyone telling me what to do," he ended.

"Which is why I left, Mark. So I wouldn't. You've got to understand that I ran off because there are places I don't belong in your life." Mark tried to deny it, but she cut him off. "Think about it. I'm right and you know it."

"What you're doing, in none-too-subtle terms, is asking me to go back home, to New York."

"Yes." Tempering his mood, Mark fiddled with the stem of his water glass and stared at the gleaming, white china plate where his dinner would soon be served. Gwynn looked stricken, so he added, "It's not that I don't enjoy seeing you. I simply want to make this decision without being distracted."

"Is that what I am, Knucklehead? A distraction?"

"Yes."

"Ummmm. I don't know whether to punch you or hug you."

Mark laughed. "I stir those kinds of reactions in women."

"No kidding."

Sullen atmosphere enveloped them. The last time he had taken Gwynn to The Chestnut Street Grill, their relationship had been on an entirely different plane. Passion and romance had held them enthralled. Desires had run rampant. As far as Mark could tell, they both seemed to realize the fact that there would be no thunder and lightning between them. Not anymore.

Still, he couldn't for the life of him figure out why. She was as attractive as ever, and just as appealing as he remembered. Why couldn't he get excited about seeing her again, or starting a relationship?

"You're staying."

Puzzled, Mark gave her a blank look. "What? No, not necessarily. I haven't made up my mind yet."

Her perfectly shaped fingers did a slow circle around the mouth of her wineglass while a waiter delivered two orders of Calamari. "I have the feeling I should apologize for barging into town. I guess I don't belong here anymore. With you especially."

He wanted to soothe troubled waters by denying her honest remark, but to do so would have been a disservice to them both. Gwynn deserved as much truthfulness in return.

"I'm afraid that's true. At least we've found out for sure. You and I were quite a team when we were together, but that part of our lives is over with. There's nothing bad, or final in that. If I end up in New York, I'll be counting on you to help me out."

Gwynn sighed in a shaky way, pushing back her hair and settling into her chair more comfortably. "Then maybe this trip was for the best."

"To clear the air?"

Gwynn nodded. "But I'm still hoping you leave Chicago. You'll knock 'em dead in New York. You're a hell of a writer. That may not have been the reason I came to Chicago, Mark, but that's what it comes down to. You deserve to be among the very best in your field."

Insight bathed him like a sunbeam. Mark stared at her, struck by how suddenly the situation with *Sports Illustrated* became a settled matter. Amazing, he thought. There was only one way to go now. In an instant, after all the haggling he had done of late, Mark made his decision about the job offer.


Two days later, when she returned to her desk from a trip to the copy machine, Jennifer found a folded, half-slip of paper perched on top of her desk. Her name had been scrawled across the front.

The writing was familiar. A smile dawned when she opened the paper and read,

> Jennifer Marie Meyers
> You Are Cordially Invited For:
> Dinner, Wine, and Countless
> Reruns of *I LOVE LUCY*
> Time: 6:30   Place: *Where Else?*
> RSVP-Mark Abington

Just for fun she used the phone, to be very official, and watched him answer the call through the open entryway of his office. They smiled at each other.

"Well?" he asked post haste.

"I accept your invitation. Can I bring anything?"

She always asked, Mark thought. Never once had they shared a dinner, at her apartment or his home, without making it a cooperative event. "The wine."

"And dessert. Cheese cake."

She laughed when Mark grinned and said, a la Ricky Ricardo, "Aw, Luuuzeee!"


"Rickyyyyy! Ricky, wait for *me!*" There was a necessary, meaningful pause as Lucy eyed the camera in desperation, her eyes misting over at a misbegotten deed. "Waaaaaahhhhh!"

Side by side on the couch in Mark's living room, he and Jennifer erupted into the kind of unbridled, spontaneous laughter that Lucille Ball alone could inspire.

During the writing of Mark's book about Phil Jackson, they had discovered a mutual passion for the *I Love Lucy* show. Since then, they had gone so far as to video tape some of their favorite episodes and currently watched one of the cassettes they had pieced together.

Now, the tape they viewed faded to static and their laughter echoed into silence.

Retrieving her goblet of wine from the coffee table, Jennifer turned toward Mark. She curled her legs beneath her. Rolling the stem of the glass between her hands, Jennifer observed the dark red liquid as it washed the bowl of the goblet in thick waves.

Quietly, Mark let loose a bombshell. "I'm staying on at the *Sentinel*."

*Hallelujah!* Jennifer's relief came immediately but she worked hard to keep her face impassive. "When did you decide?"

"I made it official this afternoon. Tom and I inked a deal late today, and the paper gave me a great contract. S.I. doesn't know yet. They'll find out from my agent in the morning. After Tom, I wanted you to be the first to know."

Jennifer waited for more, eyeing him suspiciously as he went to the tape player and turned it off. *"And . . . !"*

Mark turned and cracked a large smile. "And I'm happy. I feel good. Peaceful. The *Sentinel* made me a terrific deal . . ."

"What about *you*, Abington?" Jennifer interrupted. "To heck with *deals*. You're the bottom line."

"No, the bottom line is my salary, Face." He rejoined her at the couch. "It happens to be great."

"Oh, good. I'm glad your priorities are straight."

"I feel content. I made the right decision. Chicago is where I belong. Maybe later I'll make a move, but not now. I'd be miserable in New York."

Still Jennifer was skeptical. She pursed her lips, studying Mark. "Answer one more question then I'll feel better."

"Yes, madame reporter."

"How much did Kevin and Gwynn have to do with this speedy decision?"

"Absolutely nothing." Dramatically he clutched his heart. "Scout's honor."

Across the back of the couch, he reached for her hand and linked his fingers through hers. Jennifer felt her body go pliant, and had to suppress a desire to move in close and snuggle next to his body. Receptors went to work, powerful in that she felt his touch with astounding clarity. If only she could lay next to him in bed, like she had the night her father died, and drift sweetly to sleep while cuddled in the warmth of his arms.

"I want to talk about Kevin, Jen." He stopped there, receiving her nod of ascent. "To be brutally honest, he's jealous of me. He's riding me because he's under the impression that you and I are developing a romantic relationship."

Jennifer swallowed hard, felt her eyes widen. In truth, she didn't know what stunned her more, hearing her unspoken thoughts take voice or discovering that Kevin Owens still carried a torch. Well it could burn down to his fingertips for all she cared.

*"What?"* She felt herself start to stammer. "He . . . thinks . . . he's jealous? Of . . . of . . ."

Releasing her hand, Mark slid his knuckles against her cheek. "That's right, Face. He's determined we're an item. That's what's making him so possessive and even angry."

Jennifer felt her heart twist. The idea of a romance between them seemed ludicrous to Mark, and that hurt. A lot. Absorbing the tender stroke of his fingers against her skin made Jennifer want to writhe. Restless, sensual energy wrapped around her, enticing and undeniable. *Futile.*

"Guess that's a pretty preposterous idea," she said softly, looking at the floor. She felt ashamed of herself for letting passion ruin what had been a perfect friendship.

Unfortunately, Mark didn't disagree. "Yes it is. Considering how close we are, who needs the hassle?" Pausing a beat he asked, "Right?"

How she kept from crying, Jennifer had no way of knowing. The evening, she felt, had just come to a screeching halt. Wrapping rejection around her like a coat, she stood from the couch, stretched, and acted as casual as her wounded heart would allow.

"Keep Kevin in line for me, Mark," she said in an off-hand manner, reaching for her purse. "As for me, don't worry. I learn from my mistakes." *All of them.*

She got no further than two steps from the couch. Lightning quick, Mark stood and spun her around by taking her hand. "Hey . . . hey . . ."

He curved a finger beneath her chin, forcing her gaze to meld with his. *Those fingers,* she thought disparagingly, *they're so innocent and caring. But they do a number on my mind now.*

Being with him made her feel greedy. She wanted all of him now—not just his friendship, but his love as well. How could she back away from him now and be happy again?

"As usual, I no sooner get on track with you than something goes wrong. You closed in on me like a steel vault just now, Face. What happened to you?"

"Nothing!" Oh, damn, she cursed silently, why did I shout? Talk about incrimination!

He moved close. The length of their bodies touched, just barely.

The musky scent of his body surrounded her with heat, forcing surrender, making denial impossible.

"Jennifer, what did I do wrong? I wasn't rebuking you." His voice lowered in pitch, going from warm and low to smoke and satin. "You're precious to me, Face. If you need proof, I'll admit something—you're one of the main reasons I'm staying."

Hope renewed, she held her breath, awaiting each word.

"I couldn't leave Chicago," he continued. "There are a lot of people here who are special to me, you being chief among them."

One of a throng. Crumpling on the inside, Jennifer felt like screaming at the injustice of it all. *Mark*, she told him silently, *my feelings run deeper than that. I don't want to lose you, but I'm not happy just being your buddy anymore.*

Mark couldn't make heads or tails of her mood right now. Sensing her confusion, he tried to comfort Jennifer by offering her the assurance of his touch, hoping to communicate his feelings.

Cupping her face between his hands, Mark caressed her cheeks with the pad of his thumbs. She slid her hands over his with a shaky smile.

"Sorry I'm acting weird," she excused feebly. "I'll be honest, too. I thought the offer from S.I. would be too good for you to pass up. I'm glad you'll be here." But that wasn't even *half* the truth.

Smiling, a teasing light in his eyes, he did a Ricky Ricardo impersonation. "Thanks, Luuuzee . . ."

The kiss took her by surprise.

He spoke, then his head dipped low. Gently his mouth captured hers, making his love and affection plain. This was the kiss of a friend, Jennifer knew, yet the warmth of his mouth against hers made her insides turn languorous. Her skin burned. She nearly sighed with need, thinking, *Can he feel my heart pound?*

His kiss, so tender and soft, was like tasting a dream and letting it seduce her, only to have the sweetness disappear like flavor itself once he pulled away.

She wanted more. She wanted to feel his arms slide around her. She wanted him to press her limp body against the hardness of his. She wanted the moist, hot touch of his tongue against her teeth. Her body throbbed, needing release from the tension he stirred.

Looking at her, Mark saw the disappointment, registered her longing, but couldn't bring himself to believe she was so shaken by his kiss. Not after how they had just defined their relationship. If she wanted more than friendship, why had she agreed to his terms?

Quickly Jennifer composed herself, assuming a casual air. She raked back the side of his hair in an affectionate way. "See you tomorrow."

"And for a long time afterward, Face. I'm here to stay."

## Eight

Mark went to his car in the parking lot of the *Sentinel,* barely noticing the note and flower that had been pinned beneath the wiper blades of the windshield.

He stored his lap-top computer and briefcase in the back seat of his car and was about to toss his suit coat next to it when he stopped short, seeing the delivery.

The sight of a pale pink envelope and vivid white rose brought a wry smile to his face. Mark spied his name written across the envelope and shook his head. Receiving gifts and letters wasn't an unheard of experience for him considering the high profile of his job, but they made him feel uncomfortable to a degree, like he was receiving something he didn't deserve.

For now, though, he was in a hurry to get to Chicago Stadium and interview a few Bulls players before tonight's basketball game.

The Bulls were nearing the end of their season with an outstanding record, so play-off mania had begun to grip the Windy City. As a result of the Bulls' good fortune, and since Mark had decided to continue as lead sports columnist at the newspaper, Tom Brewer had recently announced a college-wide search for a Production Assistant.

The production assistant would help Mark by doing leg-work and research during the NBA semi-finals and, hopefully, the championship series. Over the next few days, Tom would do preliminary interviews. After narrowing down the choices, Mark would be called upon to help pick the person they ultimately hired.

So, with much on his mind, Mark didn't have time right now to deal with a fan letter. He set the flower on the seat next to him and slipped the note into the side pocket of his jacket. Driving to the stadium, he focused on the game to come.

Returning home afterward, when he hung up his suit coat, a crinkle of paper reminded him of the note he hadn't yet read. Taking the envelope, he went to the kitchen to make himself a cup of hot tea in the microwave.

Sliding his thumbnail beneath the seal of the envelope, Mark pulled a matching piece of blush colored stationary from inside. As expected, the paper was full of what looked like a woman's delicate, fine script.

Mark-

I'm incredibly nervous about writing you this letter. You have no idea how difficult I find it to put my feelings into words . . . onto paper . . . even with the veil of anonymity I choose to wear.

Yes, I admire you—as you can tell by the way I've signed the end of this letter and the simple, fragrant beauty of the rose I have included. But please Mark, before you surrender to the temptation you may have to toss this letter away unread, I want you to realize something. We know one another. Very well, actually.

As I write these lines, I tremble, recalling the times we have shared. I close my eyes and I feel the touch of your fingertips against my cheek. I breathe and I'm suddenly next to you, the spice of your cologne teasing my senses.

I'll end this note now. I need you to have it as soon as possible. If I delay in this, if I give in to the doubts and fears I have about approaching you, I'll remain forever silent.

I'll be in touch with you again soon. And know, wherever you may be, that I think of you lovingly.

Until we meet again . . .
Your Admirer

The microwave bell sounded, but Mark didn't hear. He stared at the paper he held, feeling unnaturally warm. His heart thudded heavily against his chest and he couldn't take his eyes from the pastel-pink colored paper he held. Re-reading the letter did something strange and unexpected—it thrummed his nerves.

*My God,* he thought, catching his breath, *I'm actually letting this get to me. I'm affected. By an admirer letter!*

Mark rebuked himself further, thinking, this woman, whoever she is, has a knack for sensuous writing, but to allow himself to get into a lather over a letter was insanity.

Considering the number of times he had dated recently, or even socialized with friends made his pattern of self-analysis darken even further. He needed to get out more, and find companionship. This state of temporary celibacy wasn't agreeing with him if something like a "secret admirer" ploy could put fire to his hormones.

He had been alone too much lately. Putting the letter on a counter next to the microwave, Mark took his tea mug and went to the living room. Trouble is, he admitted, there wasn't a woman around who ignited his needs . . . not just for sex, but for companionship as well. There wasn't a woman in his life who made him want to drop everything and spend a night at home, simply, with nothing on the agenda but each other.

No one except Jennifer.

Mark's movements froze midway between delivering his tea mug to his lips. *Jennifer?* Where had *that* thought come from?

He set the cup aside with a loud clunk. Nope, he decided immediately. No dice. She's off limits—a precious friend. Theirs was one relationship he felt determined to keep close and uncomplicated. Wonderful. Being lovers would, potentially, wreak havoc.

Jennifer Meyers and romance tallied together equalled a risk too big to take.

"I'm calling to say happy birthday to Mark."

Kevin sent a savoring look toward his colleague. Sitting next to him, Mark sighed inaudibly, his sportscast just concluded, his earphones still in place. Thinking this was just another nutty caller, Mark rolled his eyes and prepared to tolerate a ribbing from Kevin. The provocative tones of this particular lady would be too much for Kevin to ignore.

Thanks to distance, and the fact that Kevin had made no overtures toward Jennifer, Mark's relationship with him had regained a cautious type of equilibrium. Sadly, though, he no longer felt close to Kevin. Nowadays they didn't speak or see each other outside the walls of the studio. Their only contact came during the morning show, and the uneasy truce they held lacked even traces of warmth.

"Birthday greetings. How nice of you to think of him." Kevin chuckled, asking, "What's your name, sweetheart?"

"Oh . . . just call me an admirer."

Mark's ears prickled immediately. He straightened, staring at the volume monitors and the steady white light of the phone bank where the call originated.

The voice sounded like that of a fairly young woman . . . but it was low, and soft, familiar somehow, yet not quite.

"Well, thanks for the sentiment," Kevin concluded, unimpressed with that, ready to move along to other callers.

Mark grabbed his hand to stop him. "Where are you calling from?"

"Close by. It seems I have your interest, Mark."

Indeed. Instantly he associated the woman's voice with pale pink stationary, sweet roses and romantic words. The woman sounded flirtatious, the fun of teasing a man to distraction evident in her voice.

Mark's brows came together in a frown and he felt frustration seethe inside him. Oh yes, it was her all right, his secret admirer. "I want to know who you are since we've been communicating lately."

"Yes we have. Or, actually, you and your admirer have. I'm simply her envoy."

Mark groaned, the sound carrying across the airwaves.

Gleefully, Kevin jumped in at that point. "What's going on, Mark?"

"Nothing," he barked, staring at the phone line. Intrigue spurred him on. "Where is she?"

"At work," the voice answered smoothly.

Great. This person wasn't lying, but she wasn't being open, either. "She writes a great letter. Tell her that for me."

"You just did it yourself. She's listening. And she wants me to ask you if you'd like to hear from her again."

"I'd like to *meet* her," he qualified.

"Do you want to *hear* from her again?" the woman repeated.

Mark sighed inwardly. He wasn't going to get anywhere being straightforward. He tried a ploy of his own. "In person?"

"That's up to her."

No dice on that one, he thought. Match point had just been won.

"Yes," Mark surrendered unwillingly. "I'd like to hear from her again. But I want to meet her, too."

"You'll *hear* from her when you're finished at the studio."

The line went dead. Mark chewed on the inside of his cheek to keep silent. Kevin, he noticed, gaped at him, curiosity brimming.

Testimony to the gap that now yawned between them, Kevin made no move to question Mark, or treat him to a good natured teasing like he would have done before. Mark didn't know whether to be greateful for that or feel hurt at the loss of a good friend.

An hour later, in the lobby of the building, Mark was stopped on his way out. With a large smile, the middle-aged woman seated at the reception desk handed him a large bouquet of flowers. Oddly, a seductive heat spread through his body.

No sooner did he enter his car and close the door behind him than he tore off the crisp covering of green paper. He was stunned at the sight of over a dozen, long-stemmed, white roses.

And a note . . .

>Mark-
>
>Hearts are not had as a gift.
>Hearts are *earned*. Happy birthday.
>Until we meet again . . .
>
>Your Admirer

The note, on his correspondent's trademark pink stationary, made his heart pound in a strange way, and Mark knew then and there that he had to figure out who was torturing him like this.

But how? Setting the flowers aside, frustrated yet piqued, he engaged his car and drove toward the headquarters of the *Sentinel*.

When he entered his office, he was in for another surprise.

A box of chocolate turtles, his favorite candy, was rimmed by tiny, sugar hearts—the kind kids send to each other on Valentine's Day that have corny messages printed on them. All of Mark's hearts said the same thing. "Be Mine . . . "

He was in the midst of questioning everybody in the sports department about the delivery of candy that had been left on his desk, but no one knew a thing. During one such inquisition, the phone on Jennifer's desk began to buzz. She had left for the moment, so Mark picked up the receiver.

"Meyers' desk."

"Jennifer Meyers, please?"

"She's not here right now. Can I take a message?" He felt irritated at playing secretary when there was detective work to do. He tried to be professional, but it took effort.

"This is Templeton's Flower Shop, calling about the roses she ordered. We'd like to confirm that they were delivered and that she was pleased with our service."

Mark nearly dropped the phone.

"Come again?" he choked. "What did you just say?"

An exasperated sigh from the clerk didn't faze him a bit. Impatiently she repeated her statement and waited for Mark to request a return name and number. He recorded the information and hung up the receiver in a daze.

His admirer. Jennifer. Jen? *Face?*

He sank into the office chair in front of her desk and propped up his elbows. Running his fingertips lightly along a silver framed picture of Jennifer and her family, he swivelled from side to side, trying to figure out what to do.

For most of the early afternoon, he would be tied up conducting employment interviews for the new production assistant. Tom Brewer had quickly narrowed the choices down to three prospects and he now wanted Mark's input on the final decision. Damn it all. Time constraints forced him to shelve a confrontation for now . . . but not for long.

He picked up the message he had taken, and his face lit with a broad, knowing smile.

Dropping a stack of wire copy on top of her desk, Jennifer sat down, preparing to sort through current sports reports. Automatically she turned on her computer terminal and retrieved the story she had been working on before returning from a late lunch. As she punched in commands, her intercom buzzed.

"Jennifer, can I see you for a minute, please?" Mark asked, sounding extremely businesslike.

"Sure. On my way." Picking up a notepad, feeling confused by his formality, Jennifer shrugged it off and went to his office. "Hi. What's up?"

"Close the door, please."

Again with the formality, Jennifer thought, utterly puzzled. She complied and sat down. Mark stood and moved closer, propping his hip against the edge of his desk, just inches away from her.

Jennifer looked up slowly, immediately off-balance when she detected an unfamiliar glint in his eyes. "What did *I* do?"

"I appreciated the flowers, Jen."

"Flo . . . flow-ers?" she stammered, shaking her head.

Mark moved closer, not touching her, but looking her straight in the eyes. "Yes. Flowers. The roses, and my birthday chocolates."

Heightened color painted her cheeks a bright hue of pink. She blinked, trying to maintain the stare he had instigated. "But I didn't . . ."

He smiled, a wonderful, captivating smile that turned her insides over. Jennifer continued, but her voice sounded tremulous to her own ears. "No, Mark. I got you that sports almanac for your birthday, and a certificate for dinner at Planet Hollywood."

Mark just shook his head. "I've got you dead to rights, Jen. The florist called while you were away from your desk. They wanted to make sure you were happy with the roses and their delivery service."

"Oh." A slight pause followed. Jennifer treated him to a glare. "And did they say *where* they had delivered the flowers, Marcus Allen?"

His confidence faltered, but he tried not to let it show. She only called him by his full name, in that tone of voice, when she was really ticked-off, or wanted to get a rise out of him. *And he hadn't asked where the delivery had taken place.*

"Well did they?" she persisted stonily, waiting for his answer.

"Ah . . . no . . . not exac . . ."

Exasperated, she interrupted. "I ordered two dozen roses for my sister. Yesterday was *her* birthday. Stacy turned twenty and since you don't reach a milestone every day, I wanted to do something special for her. Surely you remember that coincidence—how close your birthdays are."

Something about her pat, ready answer didn't jive, but Mark couldn't figure out what. He did a silent stumble, looking at her in confusion. Jennifer stared right back, her upper-hand restored, her eyes clear and faultless. Then she smiled wickedly, like he had done earlier, and Mark felt like a total idiot.

"Mark, you didn't actually think . . . No! You didn't think your famed secret admirer was *me,* did you?"

She stood, eye to eye with him. The lines of her face were soft and sweet, and suddenly Mark was nearly overcome by an urge to kiss her arrogant looking mouth until she . . .

"I'm flattered," she said quietly, touching his face with the back of her hand. "I really am. And I do admire you, you know. But if I had . . . well . . . if I felt *those* type of feelings for you, I think we'd be able to be straight with each other and admit it. We know each other well enough for that." There was the barest hint of a pause. "Don't we?"

Every ounce of air now expelled from his theories about Jennifer, Mark could only nod dumbly. A small degree of doubt remained, but he didn't press her.

Moving close, she paused, then moved even closer and gave his cheek a quick kiss. She left his office, but Mark felt cold and sad when she was gone.

This secret admirer thing, he cursed silently, is making me nuts. It's got me edgy and stirred up.

*This has got to stop.*


Thoughts of Jennifer dominated Mark's mind as he drove home that night. After opening the front door, he knelt to retrieve the day's mail which had been deposited through the brass slot.

A pink envelope, with only his name written across the front, immediately caught his eye. Mark's pulse rate accelerated as he set aside his computer and brief case. Turning the envelope over and over, he sat down heavily on the couch. Already preparing for an onslaught of sexual energy, the muscles of his body started to coil up like thousands of tightly wrapped springs.

"Let's see what you have to say today," he muttered to the empty air. Ripping open the envelope, he pulled two sheets of paper from inside.

A scintillating aroma drifted upward, capturing his imagination, tempting the fringes of his memory.

Puzzled, he lifted the pages to his nose and inhaled the fragrance of rich, understated floral perfume. Of their own volition, his hands dropped to his lap and he groaned.

"All right, all right," he muttered, "message received."

And he began to read . . .

Mark-

Since you hit so close to home today, the time has come to be honest—for both our sakes.

Before I do, though, I want to thank you. You've held my hand, comforted me through a terrible period in my life, given me joy by just smiling, or touching me gently . . .

I slept in your arms one night and awoke feeling calm and utterly soothed. It felt right to wake up in your bed, and that stunned me. You see, I never expected to fall in love with my best friend.

The power of these feelings scares me. I feel a passion for you that I'm afraid is not returned. I've fallen in love with you, but I've been betrayed by a man I thought I loved, and I fear making another painful mistake. Fresh after I had discovered these feelings, Gwynn Aldridge paid a visit to Chicago. I wanted to believe I was being noble, defending you against a woman who wanted to manipulate you into going to New York City. That's only half the truth. The whole truth is that I want you here. With me.

Through Gwynn I discovered I would fight for our relationship if necessary.

I bluffed today, Mark. You had found me out, and I could think of only one thing as you confronted me. Escape. I'm afraid of you now, and times have changed between us because you now hold my heart.

You offer friendship and my heart has turned, my feelings have intensified to deeper levels than friendship. But I don't want to lose you.

Let me off the hook. Let's talk now. I need my peace of mind back. I need my best friend.

Love,
*Face*

Everything fell into place after that. The perfume was Jennifer's fragrance. He had noticed it several times. And the roses, he thought, feeling as though puzzle pieces were fitting together with a perfect click. They hadn't been for her sister. That's what hadn't jived about her story. Now, away from a heated battle with Jennifer, he remembered how frantic she had been trying to put together Stacy's 20th birthday party several months ago.

"Jen," he said softly, emotion coating his words, "what in the world have you been going through? Why didn't you come to me? We could have . . ."

Could have *what?* he couldn't help wondering. And, for now, he just didn't have the answer.

"Were you surprised at the stir the uniforms caused?"

There was a pause while Jennifer held her phone receiver and waited for an answer to her question. She didn't hear footfalls behind her. She was concentrating so hard that she didn't sense Mark's arrival.

"Yes," she continued, "I agree that the debut of Chicago's *Lady Rebels* basketball team was a success. The game was exciting . . . yes. I understand, but having the women wear uniforms of tight fitting spandex drew some strong reactions from some members of the team and the public."

Mark's arm formed a barricade to her left, pinning Jennifer to her desk as he leaned over her shoulder. He was so close, seemed so touchable and sexy. Jennifer shifted uncomfortably, trying to ease her reaction to him, the need she felt. It was a useless attempt. The proximity of his body, the warm, subtle scent of his skin, clouded her concentration.

Holding down the sheets of a notepad that Jennifer was trying to page through, Mark garnered her full attention. They exchanged a stare and Jennifer faltered in her conversation. Mark smiled to himself when he realized her hands were trembling. Distractedly, wanting to hide that fact, she twiddled a pen. Pulling his own pen from a shirt pocket, he ignored her now disjointed conversation with the basketball coach and reached over her shoulder to write a message.

*Get away at 4:30.*

Deliberately he held the pen out to her, waiting for Jennifer to take it, waiting for her fingertips to slide against his. He craved the physical contact with her.

Hesitantly she took the pen, studiously avoiding his eyes. Mark smiled at her shy behavior.

*Where to?* she scribbled.

*My place,* he wrote, watching her chest rise and fall. Close enough to be tantalized by the aroma of her perfume, Mark turned his head, letting his lips graze her hairline as he began to straighten up.

They passed, hours later, in a nearly deserted hallway. Mark grabbed Jennifer's hand and pushed her through the doorway of a vacant conference room. He closed the door behind them and pinned her against a wall . . . gently, though . . . with nothing more asked than that she stay put, very close by.

"I haven't had a chance to tell you how great you look."

Mark's eyes took her in, from top to bottom. A well-styled blouse of creme colored silk had chunky gold buttons that glittered in the overhead light. The long sleeves of her shirt had been rolled up to give her freedom of movement, and when he ran his hands lightly along her arms, the soft fabric slid upward . . .

He shook his head. "I should wrap my fingers very carefully around that neck of yours and strangle you, Face. You drove me nuts."

"Sorry," she whispered, looking down. She blushed.

"Is it getting to you?" he asked with equal softness, capturing her eyes with his as he touched his hand very lightly to her abdomen. "Is it hitting you right there? Like it is me?"

The affected expression on his face made her throat go dry. It's as though he can read my mind, she thought hazily, for she indeed felt her stomach go free-falling as the timbre of his voice stroked her as effectively as his fingertips.

Words escaped her. They were stolen by powerful emotions she longed desperately to express but couldn't.

At last, all she could do was nod, a last remnant of steel in her demeanor. "Don't do this to me, Mark. Please. Not here . . . not now."

Relenting, Mark backed away, opening the door for her.

"Fair enough, Jen. *Tonight.*"

# Nine

"Leave your inhibitions on the doorstep," Mark commanded lowly.

As expected, her glance fell away when she read the message being telegraphed between them. They stood at the entrance of his home, and Mark didn't let her back away. He lifted her chin with a light touch beneath her jaw.

"We're going to give it all to each other tonight," he whispered, his mood unflinching. "There will be no interruptions, no work, no games or hiding. Nothing to interfere."

"I'm nervous."

Mark shook his head to push her objection away. "Don't be, Jen." A teasing grin lit his face. "Isn't this what you were after when you devised that secret admirer seduction?" She didn't answer, but her eyes begged for his tenderness, his understanding, so he spoke his heart. "This is what we both want, so no more running. For either one of us."

Unlocking the door, Mark pushed it open, waiting for Jennifer to pass by. As she did, their bodies brushed, silk against cotton. Mark felt taut with anticipation and pleasure, the culmination of what they had found together was so close at hand. Purposefully he let his hand trail along her arm in a brief, speaking caress.

Following her inside, Mark left the lights off so his living room would be bathed in the diffused, golden light of late afternoon.

"Sit down," he instructed. "I'll get us something to drink. Does wine sound good?"

"Sure."

In the time he spent away, Jennifer paced, wishing she could ease her feelings of nervousness. Not really knowing if it was the smart thing to do, but wanting the comfort it would bring, she slipped off her black leather pumps, so she could enjoy the feel of plush carpeting beneath her stocking feet.

Mark returned, carrying two goblets of chablis wine. He sat down in front of the fireplace, putting her glass on the hearth.

Realizing that she was expected to join him, Jennifer walked tentatively to where he sat and picked up her glass, sipping the wine as their eyes dead-locked on each other.

She stood and he sat, until Mark gave a soft sigh and a smile. "Come here, sweetheart."

Nerve endings began to thrum beneath Jennifer's skin, sliding downward, to an area between her legs that always tightened and ached when he spoke to her in such a stirring, low tone. She found herself complying without even thinking about it.

"You belong here," he said, watching her steadily as she carefully folded her legs. Her shoes, he noticed, had been removed, and that pleased him. So did the sight of her polished toenails. Something about that sensual indulgence made his stomach muscles tighten with desire.

Mark took the wineglass from her hand and set both their goblets aside, wanting to surrender the pretense of casual behavior.

For the moment, he studied her face. He reached up and used the back of his knuckles to stroke the skin of her cheek. "Deep down, I knew it would be you, Jen. Even when I called your bluff on the florist, and you squirmed out of the corner I put you in, I knew it was you. Things changed for us during the time after your father died, Face. All of a sudden it's become uncomfortable to be friends." He shrugged slightly. "Friendship just isn't enough for us anymore."

Her thoughts exactly—nearly verbatim. The longings he roused within her only increased at his words.

"No, it's not," she whispered in agreement.

Tenderly, Mark combed his fingers through her hair, all the while holding her eyes hostage. But there remained a safety net of space between them and he made no move to close in.

"Lay back."

Mark's command set her heart off like a trip hammer. A tide of panic, coupled with desire and need, flushed through her body like molten liquid.

"Mark . . ." she beseeched fearfully.

Hearing the doubt in her voice, sensing and respecting her feelings, he continued to sit perfectly still, but he reached out with a hand to cup her chin.

"Lay down," he coaxed seductively, now broaching the space between them.

He slid an arm around her shoulders and guided her back. Jennifer, he felt pleased to find, surrendered willingly, laying next to him. Mark propped himself on his forearm, leaning over her in a possessive way.

"You're trembling, Face," he observed when he laced the fingers of his free hand through hers. "Trouble is, I don't want you to tremble with nerves. I don't want you to be nervous. I want you to tremble with a different emotion. Passion." He paused there, letting his words sink in. "I'm going to take the fear away. All you have to do is *let me.*"

But her skittishness wasn't gone yet, so he didn't press ahead quickly like his body urged him to do. Instead, Mark only tipped his head until his lips feather-touched the skin of her neck. Closing his eyes, he breathed in the unique scent of her skin.

Using his lips, he nuzzled her throat, her flush warmed cheeks, ever mindful to keep the caress as light as possible so it would ignite her senses.

Involuntarily, Jennifer sighed, letting her head loll weakly to the side. That gave Mark better access to the skin behind her ears, her neck . . .

Then he broke contact, looking down into her face as she turned toward him once more. For a few seconds he enjoyed simply looking into her eyes. Warm, rich colored sunlight bathed her, causing intriguing shadows and light plays. Mark released her hand and took hold of her shoulder.

She was warm to his touch, even beneath the cool, slippery fabric of her blouse. The realization made his body tighten all the more. Despite an overwhelming need, he maintained deliberation and purpose.

"Don't do a thing," he whispered, moving his hand to her neck, then to her lips so his fingertips could trace the outline of her mouth. "You're mine tonight. Completely. I don't want anything more of you than response, Jennifer. Give me yourself. That's all I want."

"But I want to make you happy," she said tremulously, her voice so husky it sounded foreign to her. "I'm no good at this, Mark." In vain she fought against the delicious flood of languor he inspired by touching her body with such care. "These feelings are new to me. I'm too overpowered to move, let alone make you feel the same kind of things for me that I do for you."

Throughout her speech, Mark had been shaking his head.

"You already make me happy," he assured firmly. "If you mean what you say, Jen, if you want to make me happy, then relax. Your mission is accomplished. Hear me?"

There would be no argument to that, he knew. It was the truth—plain, simple, and irrefutable. But he had to break down the walls of her modesty. He had meant what he said about leaving inhibitions behind, he wanted nothing at all holding her back.

Not until he was completely convinced that she would surrender to him, without doubts and fears in the way, did he say, "Let me show you what I feel. I haven't had that luxury yet."

Jennifer expected everything to happen at once after that . . . the fire, the press of his body against hers, the long desired union.

It didn't.

Mark barely moved. Instead, he slipped his hand beneath the collar of her v-neck blouse and held her neck. They shared a long, stirring kiss and Jennifer lifted her arms to hold him. After a snug, sultry hug, he pulled away, just a bit, and turned her face toward his.

He ran his hand down the front of her, to her waist, his touch made twice as sensitive by the silk shirt she wore. He drew the ends of it from the leather belt and waistband of her skirt. Stiffening momentarily, Jennifer felt him work the large, gold buttons free, slowly, one by one.

Rather than stare at her, and make her feel uncomfortable, he watched his hands as they accomplished their task. When he finished, he parted the fabric and slid it away. Jennifer's breasts were full, peaked by hardened nipples that pushed upward against her bra, calling for the touch of his lips, his tongue and fingers . . .

With deliberate movements he did away with her bra and began to sate himself with touching her. His fingertips slid along her now bare shoulder, then her arm, making her shiver with the anticipation of his touch against other, more intimate and needy places.

Next he familiarized himself with her waistline, his hands moving upward, to her ribcage. Cupping her breast, Mark molded the soft skin. He ran his thumb tip across her nipples, which evoked a soft moan from Jennifer.

All was slow motion, and arousing heat. She reached up, sinking her fingers into his hair, but didn't feel quite bold enough to bring him to her breasts. Positioning herself closer, she fit her body to his.

Jennifer's face told Mark his seduction was working, so he didn't wait for encouragement but touched the tip of one nipple with his tongue, teasing the nerve endings there with feathery strokes.

She whimpered in exclamation, taking a sharp breath of air as she arched against him. Mark took the entire nipple into his mouth, murmuring sexy love words as he suckled on her breasts with love bites that shot heat through her limbs.

"Oh, Mark . . ."

Nervousness, she realized in a blind heat, was retreating like a defeated warrior. The thick brown strands of his hair sifted through her fingers as she pressed his head to her chest, greedy for sensation, encouraging the explorations he had instigated. Between her legs, an incessant throbbing caused her to move against him.

In a deft movement, he unhooked her belt and slid it away, next unfastening the button and zipper of her skirt so he could push it away as well. His head was mere centimeters above hers, his breath warm and sweet against her face.

Dressed only in her nylons and panties, Jennifer felt her body yearn for him as he flattened his hand gently against her tummy and moved it slowly, slowly downward. A fiery tingle alerted her to an approaching catalyst, and she felt every muscle beneath his touch tighten and coil with hot tension.

Once he encountered the top band of her hose, Mark paused and looked into her eyes. Jennifer gasped softly because he didn't give her respite for long but glossed his hand lightly over her abdomen, letting his touch trail between her legs.

The clingy, thin fabric of her nylons was like a second skin. The silky material intensified his touch to a degree that Jennifer had no way of expecting. As his fingers slipped in and out, light and purposeful, the pulse between her legs erupted into spasms that rocked her body and signaled an orgasm so powerful it stunned her.

Mark felt her wetness soak the material of her hose and quickly pushed his hand inside, pressing it firmly against her so she could ride out the vibrations of her body.

My God, he thought, *I've never experienced such responsiveness, never known of a woman so eager to be made love to. Her passion is incredible.*

His touch seemed to work on her automatically, for as his hand slid deep, her legs opened instinctively, inviting him to further his explorations. Her body lifted to his when he pulled her underclothes away. Creamy moisture welcomed him, the most telling evidence of his affect on Jennifer and her state of arousal.

"Let me look at you," Mark ordered in a growl that was purely sexual. "I want to see your face when I touch you . . . when you come . . ."

Shyness reasserted itself, so Mark forced the issue by capturing her mouth and devouring her lips. His tongue snaked inside, mating with hers the way their bodies now cried to do. Moaning into her mouth, he gently opened the folds of skin between her legs.

Kissing away the tiny beads of sweat on her brows, he murmured, "Let go, Jen. Surrender. Give this to me. You have no idea what passion you possess, how seductive you are. Don't deny yourself anything . . ."

Encouraging her further, Mark's fingers trailed repeatedly against her warm, dewy cleft. Jennifer held tightly to his shoulders, her eyes trapped by his, her every reaction, as he had wanted, now plain to see.

Lifting her lower body to him, Jennifer responded without forethought of anything but release and a desire to end the agony of need that held her mind, heart, and body captive.

"I'm not going to last . . ." she whimpered.

Mark only stepped up his caressing explorations, letting her rub and press against his palm. Now bathed with her inner cream, his fingers slipped into an even deeper caress. He maneuvered his fully clothed body against hers, kissing her deeply, with open mouthed hunger.

Immediately he felt the spasms of a second orgasm ripple through her.

He was engorged, painfully confined, and Mark drew back, greateful she had found release so quickly. Now to bring her back again . . . and finally be one with her.

He nuzzled her, as he had at the start, trailing his lips along her skin, this time letting his tongue taste the flavor of her as well. Murmuring his approval, Mark moved away so he could take off his shirt.

Although her body was temporarily spent, Jennifer watched him in fascination, realizing an emptiness at the core of her. A remnant need swelled within her, and would be eased only when their bodies were joined.

The removal of his clothing took only a few graceful moves. He stood, to peel off his suit pants and everything else he wore. The vision of his shadowed silhouette made her swallow hard. How had she lived without him as both lover and friend? she wondered fleetingly. I'll never, ever be happy without him. Sighing, Jennifer welcomed the feel of his hot, bare skin against hers as he knelt between her legs.

There was too much pent up inside Mark for him to hold off for long. She reached down, to guide and touch him, but he caught her hand with a firm rebuke. "Touch me and it's over, Jen. I'm only human."

He entered her with a powerful thrust, fitting into Jennifer's body in a tight, custom-designed way that brought tears to her eyes. Mark seemed to sense them as they moved in time together, for he licked her tears away, kissing her eyes closed as they lifted, slid, and thrust in unison.

After such shattering responses to him already, Jennifer didn't expect that final, blissful release to sweep over her so quickly, or with so much power. She curved her legs around his body, filled by him at last.

At that moment, Mark spilled into her, warm and sticky, creating a mingled moistness between her legs as they shared the last seconds of their lovemaking.

Only then did she feel utterly at peace and satisfied.


"Who called the radio station on my birthday?" he asked, a smile of memory curving his lips.

Jennifer smiled as well, laughed as they looked into each other's eyes. His voice sounded rough and sleepy, appealing. Side by side, still stretched out on the carpet, Mark had covered their naked bodies with a quilt because Jennifer had refused to move.

"My sister, Stacy," she answered. "She was my 'envoy.' "

"No wonder she sounded so familiar—she's got your voice, but there was just enough of a difference to throw me off."

"My intention exactly."

That gave him the perfect opening to ask a question that had plagued him since last night. "But why the ruse? We could have talked. You didn't need to go through all this."

Somberly she replied, "Yes I did, Mark." He was about to object but she silenced him by pressing a finger against his lips. "Hear me out. I faced the prospect of losing a friend. Correction. Not just a friend—my *best* friend. What I did, what we've done today, is an incredible risk, Mark. And I still get butterflies, thinking about starting a romantic relationship again."

"Thanks to Kevin." When Jennifer nodded, Mark groaned, rolling to his back. He stared at the ceiling, pursing his lips thoughtfully. "I knew how badly he hurt you, but I didn't think he was much of a factor anymore."

"He's not," Jennifer hastened to say. "Kevin isn't the problem, but what he did to me still is. I'm afraid of giving my heart away again. Add that to the fact that I could very well lose a fantastic friend . . ." Intentionally she let the sentence hang there, unfinished.

"Understandable." Grinning, he rolled to her. "But not anymore. This is the start of something beautiful. I know that without a doubt. Trust me, Face. I'll never deceive you, or betray your love for me."

Smiling, utterly content, she whispered, "Say that again, Marcus Allen."

"What?"

"Love."

A gentle tug brought their bodies into full contact. He growled, at once possessive and passionate. "I love you, Jennifer Marie Meyers." His eyes narrowed, boring into hers. "And don't you ever forget it."

Provocative and sexy, she rubbed her body against his. Wrapping her arms securely around his neck, Jennifer pulled him close. "Who me? Forget that? Not a prayer, *buddy*."

Their mouths melted together like hot wax, pliant and alluring. In the throes of renewed desire, Mark's body enveloped hers. Her sigh of pleasure died against the assault of his kiss. Jennifer went lax and submissive . . . welcoming Mark home.


Later that evening, curled up in bed together, Jennifer asked, "How are we going to handle things at work?"

Unperturbed, Mark reached into a cut-glass bowl of frozen grapes that rested between them. Unrepentant and unbearably provocative, he leaned on his elbow and took the plump, red fruit he held, sliding it lightly down her throat, through the valley between her breasts.

"The perfect accessory!" he exclaimed, placing the fruit in her belly button. Playful, he had a mini-feast, making her shiver and squeal as he lifted the grape from its resting place with his tongue and ate away.

"Stop that!"

"What? Me? I'm innocent, Face."

Scornful yet loving, she brought his head up, so she could look into his eyes. "Sure you are, Abington." She put the bowl on the floor. "Enough of that distraction. Answer my question."

She was genuinely concerned so Mark turned serious as well. "I'm not sure. Are you worried about Tom, and the people we work with at the paper?"

"In a way, yes. There's no policy against employees at the *Sentinel* having relationships, but I don't want anyone feeling awkward around us. I think Tom would be concerned. You're his lead sports columnist. Tremendously popular, too. He's not going to want a colleague like myself having the potential to set you off-balance professionally."

Mark looked at her steadily, silence filling the air. "You've got a point." He offered, "It might be more comfortable for everyone if we kept this to ourselves for the time being. It's no one else's business anyhow."

"I think so, too."

"Good. That decided . . ." Pinning Jennifer to the bed, he leaned over her and reached for the bowl of frozen grapes. "I want to get back to Fashion Design, 101."

He came at her with a grape and Jennifer giggled, exclaiming, "Marcus Allen! Don't you dare! . . ."

# Ten

"Samantha Malone, I'd like you to meet Jennifer Meyers. Jen is one of our staff writers."

Mark made the congenial, requisite introductions. Doing her best not to appear surprised, Jennifer stood from her desk to greet the *Sentinel's* new Production Assistant. "It's good to meet you, Samantha. Welcome aboard."

"Thank you." Despite her formal reply, Samantha's eyes were bright with anticipation and an eager desire to get off on the right foot with her colleagues. She readily accepted Jennifer's outstretched hand. "I'm looking forward to working here. And, please, call me Sam."

Jennifer accepted that with a nod and a smile, studying the woman from top to bottom. The *woman*. Strange. For all his involvement in the hiring process, Mark had failed to say anything about the fact that the position had even been filled.

Looking at Samantha, the word attractive came immediately to mind. Tall and slim, with a straight line of pale blond hair that fell just below her chin, she had natural good looks and a smile that charmed. Mostly, though, Jennifer couldn't help admiring Samantha's voice. Low and appealing, it had a tone that belonged on TV or radio voice-overs.

"She's attending school at Northwestern," Mark supplied.

"What do you study?"

"Journalism." She laughed in a self-deprecating way. "In my spare time, anyhow. My full-time endeavor is raising my son. Joshua."

*Married!* Oddly that realization gave Jennifer a rush of relief.

Smiling in a more genuine way now, Jennifer asked, "How old is your son, Sam?"

"Seven going on 40."

Mark chuckled. "Typical comment from a parent."

Samantha didn't laugh quite as sincerely, though. "True, but I'm afraid in his case, I'm not joking. I'm divorced, so for the most part, I've had to raise him on my own. Unfortunately he's pretty mature for his age."

Jennifer felt her heart plummet. *Divorced? Available?* Damn. Thoughts of Gwynn, Brenda and Kevin took root in her mind like weeds, promptly overpowering her logic.

Additionally, and setting matters even more off center, Samantha gave Mark a teasing look. "Here's an example. The first question from my beloved son's mouth once he knew I had the job was 'You're working with Mark Abington during the NBA finals, right? Does that mean I get front row seats to the games?' " Rueful, she groaned. "Seven going on 40. Wait till you meet him. Then you'll understand."

"Sounds like a pistol," Mark agreed.

"Loaded and ready to fire."

For her part, Jennifer hadn't gotten past the point in the conversation when Samantha had said, *"wait till you meet him."* Meet him? Dumfounded, feeling about as necessary to this exchange as the proverbial fifth wheel, Jennifer hoped Samantha wasn't an adept mind reader. *What are you planning on, Sam? A cozy, family dinner for three some night? Cool it!*

But Samantha Malone was a dynamo. This woman, Jennifer thought, positively commands any situation she's put in. The strong, confident way she presented herself was dazzling. A feeling of intimidation pressed down on her shoulders, unescapable and awful.

Working quickly to regroup, Jennifer gritted her teeth and forced a smile toward her new colleague while she tried desperately to push aside old, haunting fears. "I should get back to my story. Sam, I look forward to working with you."

*And discovering what you're all about,* she added in silence, still studying the woman and trying to reserve judgment.


Over lunch that afternoon, Jennifer broached the subject of Samantha Malone with Mark.

"Seems like you picked a winning Production Assistant in Samantha Malone," she observed. "She's a dynamo."

"Perfect description. I'm impressed by her. She's a bit of an overachiever, but that's understandable, considering the fact that she's a single working mother."

"Absolutely. She's anxious to get everyone on her side."

Mark set his sandwich down with a slow, deliberate movement. "That sounds an awful lot like a left-handed compliment."

"Maybe it is. You see, I'm confused."

"About what?"

"About why you didn't tell me you had filled the position, and with a woman."

Mark's jaw dropped. "First of all, I didn't hire her, *Tom* did. I simply endorsed the choice. Secondly, I didn't feel it was necessary to specify that she was a woman. What difference does *that* make? In *anything?*"

She flinched and Mark found a measure of victory in the fact that she couldn't refute his statement. Nope. She'd just have to try being honest—both with herself and with him. He knew exactly what was eating at her, but Jennifer would have to be the one to come forward and admit to jealousy and past hurt.

Intentionally pushing her, he demanded, "I'm waiting for an answer. You know, it seems we just went down this road when Gwynn came to town. What I didn't realize then is that you were jealous of her. Now I know better. This bothers you. Why?"

"I never said anything was wrong," Jennifer replied, knowing she sounded terse.

"Oh. Then I'll be equally as graceful and admit that you didn't *quite* accuse me of hiring Samantha for purely sexual reasons. Maybe we should just let the issue drop."

Jennifer's doubts remained, however, shading her eyes. Finally, after a lengthy, tense silence, she said, "You never told me about her. I wish you would have. Then I would have been prepared."

"Prepared for *what*, Face? She's a P.A. That's all. What's the big deal?" He clearly enunciated those four words, then he was even more blunt. "Or do I even need to ask. The name Kevin Owens is written all over this conversation and I don't like it. Do you?"

Helpless, Jennifer's troubled gaze fixed on him. "No, but she sparkles, Mark. Therefore, excuse me if I seem jealous and clinging for saying this, but she reminds me of Brenda."

Mark tried to eat some lunch but couldn't. To ease the negativity that had befallen their meal, he changed the subject to the inevitable spring-time topic of NBA basketball.

Still, he couldn't help thinking, *Sam puts her in mind of Brenda. That I can deal with. But does Jennifer think I'm a carbon copy of Kevin?*

The next day, Jennifer's disposition did a further nose-dive when she passed in front of Mark's office. He was in the midst of a meeting with Samantha and they were making plans for the NBA finals, should the Chicago Bulls make it that far.

". . . don't start worrying about shifting around your schedule until we know for sure that we have to travel out west. The Bulls could get eliminated in the semi-finals, but I doubt it. I'm just warning you to be prepared."

Jennifer listened to the words as she sat down at her desk. *Travelling together?* Of course. She should have assumed that. After all, that was one of the main purposes of hiring a production assistant, to give Mark and several other staff members a boost of help in covering the NBA finals for the *Sentinel*.

She heard Samantha speak up. "Nothing would keep me from L.A., or Portland in two weeks. What a thrill! I hope the Bulls make it that far."

"Are you sure you can adapt your son's schedule if need be?"

Confidence shone in Samantha's tone. Though her back was to the door, Jennifer could almost envision Samantha tossing back that shiny cap of blond hair, being mesmerizing without even realizing it.

*Or maybe, like Brenda, she did know how powerful a tool her personality was.*

"I've got parents nearby who help me out with Josh. They understand how important this job is to me, and they've always been supportive, especially where their grandson is concerned."

Jennifer didn't miss the telling catch in Samantha's voice. She didn't get the impression that Samantha's divorce was recent, but the pain it had caused obviously lingered.

Answering that Mark said, "You must feel good about having Josh in that kind of situation. With doting grandparents, I mean."

"Not really. He needs a father, or, at the very least, a father figure to look up to. Sometimes it drives me crazy that I can't do it all."

"School, work, motherhood. I'd say you're an admirable lady, Sam. Don't get down on yourself."

Shyly she laughed. "I won't. Being insane helps some, but I want him to have a man in his life that he can look up to. A father figure. That's one category I'm sorely lacking in."

Jennifer found it difficult to breathe. Her chest constricted tightly. Although they were dry, her eyes stung.

Mark and Samantha came through the doorway of his office.

"I appreciate your lunch offer," Jennifer heard her say.

"My pleasure. I know how difficult it is to be in uncharted territory. The new kid."

They passed by Jennifer's desk and something about seeing them side by side caused the devil in her soul to rise up. "Sam, I was thinking, the name Malone sounds familiar." That was a bald faced lie. Pointedly her glance sealed with Mark's. "Do you happen to have a sister named Brenda?"

Unseen by Samantha, Mark understood the entendre and glared.

Innocent to the inter-play, Samantha simply smiled and shook her head. "Afraid not. I'm a one and only."

They walked away together and Jennifer felt her spine go rigid. Clutching her purse, she crossed to Kylie's desk and took her friend by the arm. "Come here."

In an abandoned conference room, Jennifer closed the door behind them and sank into a nearby chair. "We need to talk."

Kylie sat down as well. "About Mark?" she asked slyly. Jennifer gaped and she went on to say, "Don't look so surprised. You're obvious. You should have seen your face just now when she started talking about her son, and travelling with Mark. You were so flushed, I thought you had contracted the world's worst case of flu. And I won't even mention your referral to Brenda. That was quite a slam." Teasing, she grinned. "So confess. What's going on between you and your *buddy?*"

Up until now, Jennifer thought, a week of lover's bliss.

"Believe it or not," she answered tetchily, "Mark and I are still friends. We've simply . . . ah . . ." What a time to stumble for words . . .

"Become lovers as well?" Kylie supplied, still grinning merrily.

Jennifer hissed an expletive, standing up so she could pace. "Glad you're enjoying this, Masterson. I need a friend and you're gloating."

Leaning her elbows on the table and propping her chin, Kylie offered her friend a dreamy look. "Not gloating, dear, living vicariously. How *delicious*. You? And Mark? *Perfect*. He's gorgeous, and you're ideal for him. 'Bout time you two figured that out."

Arching a brow, Jennifer turned from her contemplation of awards and pictures on the wall. "Oh really? Well Samantha Malone has blown into town with quite a bit of moxie, don't you think?"

Kylie seemed nonplussed. "Maybe, but she won't score with Mark, so get that thought right out of your piddley little brain, Jennifer. He's loyal to a fault, and . . ."

Jennifer immediately cut her off. "I *know*, Kylie!"

"But it still rankles you," she remarked compassionately. "Doesn't it?"

Jennifer didn't bother with a token denial.

Kylie continued. "She's been here a grand total of two days, Jen. Granted, she's taking the sports department by storm, but she's no threat. Not like Brenda."

"How can you say that with such confidence, Kylie?"

An understanding, half-smile curved her lips. "Because Mark Abington isn't Kevin Owens."

Kylie made an excellent point, but Jennifer didn't feel entirely comforted. A threat to her peace of mind had settled in at the *Sentinel*. Samantha Malone made her want to run for cover because she had travelled the path of betrayal before and desperately wanted to avoid a second go-round.

Jennifer sat down again. "I hate the thought of those two being colleagues in arms if the Bulls make it to the finals."

"Don't be. Enjoy what you have. If you ask me, I think you've hit the romance jackpot. I'm happy for you, Jen. No wonder you and Mark have been so starry eyed lately."

"Oh we have not." But Jennifer blushed all the same.

"Why so secretive?"

"For safety's sake. As far as our professional reputations go, we don't want anything to change just because we're together."

"Good idea." Promptly she giggled. "So why have you told me, Meyers?"

Exchanging a fond look with her friend, Jennifer answered, "Good question, Masterson. Very good question."

* * *

"What in *hell* was the meaning behind that crack about Brenda? I thought we had settled this issue at lunch yesterday."

Hours had passed, but Mark, it seemed, had counted the minutes until he could have a moment alone with Jennifer to talk about her reactions to Samantha Malone. She refused to apologize.

"Settled for *you* maybe. Not me. Something about her pushes my buttons, Mark."

"Like?"

"Like how hot blooded she gets around you."

"Jennifer!"

She didn't back away. "I'm curious about Samantha. It's interesting to me that she'll be following you out west if the Bulls make the finals. Pretty cozy. And that's something else you hadn't mentioned to me."

Mark wouldn't dignify that with an answer. "You're above being this petty."

"First you didn't tell me you had hired a female production assistant, then you didn't tell me about travelling together. Why?"

Shrugging, he tossed up his hands. "Why would travelling together matter? Obviously, as a PA she'll be acting as a gopher when the *Sentinel* has big events to cover. Lord's sake, grow up!"

"She's a steam-roller!"

"Jennifer, credit me with more sense, and more professionalism than to hire a woman to take her to bed. That may sit well with men like Kevin, but not me. You should know that without being told."

They had started to yell. Garnering her disposition, forcing herself to stay icy and calm, Jennifer replied, "You may not be able to avoid her if you want to, Mark. Just like Kevin and Brenda. Believe it or not, he wasn't entirely to blame. Remember this, *friend,* it takes *two* to tango."

Never had Mark expected such violence, such cutting behavior from Jennifer. This situation had gone way beyond simple arguments or misunderstanding. Fuming, his teeth clenched, he asked, "How can you say that? You don't even know her! You're not a witch, Jennifer, so why are you acting like one?"

"Because I feel threatened!" Closing her arms across her chest

Jennifer flopped into the chair in front of his desk, giving him a helpless look. If only she could make him understand what she felt.

"Which, as I said before, is exactly why I didn't tell you about her." Mark sat down in the chair next to hers. "I knew you'd feel this way. Needlessly, I might add. Although I never thought your anger would be this powerful."

She wasn't appeased by the tenderness of his voice. "Let's just leave it be for now. You're right, I've only known her for a few days. I'm being silly."

"No feelings you have are silly to me, Jen. All I want is to know where they come from."

"Where do you think?"

"Kevin."

"Of course."

Silence held sway. Mark moved his knee, nudging her leg gently. He leaned toward her. "I realize that, Jen. Therefore, trust me enough to have faith that I won't do that to you. I won't give you cause to doubt me. I'm yours."

She gave him a timid smile, took hold of his hand. "I like the sound of that, Abington."

He heard the telling vibration of her voice. "Don't be jealous of her. Feeling envy in the face of everything we share doesn't just hurt you, it hurts me, too."

That point of view made her feel even more foolish for blowing up. Mark kissed the palm of her hand and she felt a tingle shoot straight up the length of her arm. At this moment, she would have trusted him anywhere, anyhow, with anyone. Including Samantha Malone.

"I'll try my best," she vowed, watching his lips graze over the soft, sensitive skin. "But for me, trust comes hard."

"I understand."

As his tongue moved slowly across her palm, she caught her breath, whispering, "I don't want to mess this up."

"Me either, Face." Cockily, he winked, speaking between brushes of his mouth against her hand. "Know what? There's an all night *I Love Lucy* fest going on tonight."

She grinned right back at him, knowing exactly what was coming. "Oh? Where?"

"My place . . ."

But before their *Lucy* show marathon, Mark wanted to finish some unsettled business with Kevin Owens.

It was already late afternoon, so Mark knew Kevin would have long since left the studios of WCIO.

The next most obvious place to find him would be at home, which was located in a condominium complex just outside the city limits of Chicago.

Keeping the sparks of his anger alive, Mark thought of Jennifer and her sudden phobia of other women. It had started with Gwynn, before he had understood the depth of Jennifer's feelings. Now, Samantha's arrival at the newspaper had caused a second, even more volatile reaction. Kevin's negligence had cost Jennifer more dearly than Mark had ever realized.

This conversation, Mark decided, was long over due.

Flipping his keys around the end of his fingers, Mark walked up the sidewalk to Kevin's front door and rang the bell. Try though he might, he couldn't remember the last time nervousness had made him feel so jumpy. Perhaps his first interview, or the daunting specter of his first official deadline, or his first days at a premiere newspaper like the *Sentinel*. Gut wrenching anxiety cued him in on how meaningful this meeting was. Like it or not, Kevin was a close, long time friend, a person whose life history mirrored Mark's own.

Kevin pulled open the door with an expectant look on his face. A questioning scowl dawned almost immediately. "Hey Mark."

"Hi." They studied each other with suspicion. "Can I come in?"

Kevin didn't answer, he simply stood back and opened the door just wide enough for Mark to squeeze in.

"I hadn't expected warmth," Mark muttered, "but civility would be nice."

"Why? What do we have to say to each other?"

Mark's footsteps stalled dead center of Kevin's foyer. Slowly he turned. "You're the second person I've said this to today. *Grow up*. Treat me with the respect I deserve. You and I have been through a lot together, Kevin. Don't we owe our friendship a deeper debt than this kind of hostility? You got rid of Jennifer when she didn't suit your purposes and now you're doing the same thing to me. Well I'm

# FRIENDS AND LOVERS                                    113

here to say stop it. People aren't dispensable. It's about time you learned that. Each time you turn your back and vanish, people get hurt."

Throughout the verbal lashing, Kevin's eyes had opened wide, his temperament cooling off in the face of Mark's accusations.

"Don't tell me to get lost, or go to hell either. I came over here for one reason alone—to clear the air. You've been one of my closest friends for over a decade. Screw fifteen years of friendship? Is that what you want? If it is, fine. If it's not, then re-think the way you're living your life."

Kevin, meanwhile, had regained his composure. "You sanctimonious jerk! Where do you come off storming in here and harping at me about my life?"

"Because it's hurting Jennifer, it's hurting me, and chances are it'll end up hurting Brenda, and, yeah, even *you* before too long. You're my friend, Kevin. Nothing has changed that. Closeness, even in the past tense, gives me a license to bitch."

"Like hell," he grumbled, turning his back.

But thus far, Kevin hadn't drummed him out. Mark followed him into the living room. He continued the conversation with the force of a sledgehammer. "I am being sanctimonious. I'll admit it. But I want you to face facts. You're listening to your hormones instead of your common sense. Keep doing that, pal, and you'll end up alone. Think about it."

Kevin didn't sit. Either did Mark. Like soldiers they faced off, eye to eye in the middle of Kevin's home. "What brings this on, Mark. Jennifer?"

"No. *You.* You've been acting cruel lately and that's an anomaly. Don't forget, I know you well. Jealousy and the vindictiveness you've shown toward me lately aren't at all common to you. What brings on my sudden tangent is the fact that you're my friend."

Silence fell between them like dead weight.

"Well I haven't exactly enjoyed being on needles with you." Kevin spoke the words reluctantly, at a loud decibel.

"I'm not asking for over night change, Kevin, especially between you and me. But know this—the way you're treating people right now is going to cost you dearly." With that, Mark turned and went to the door. He had said his piece. Now it was Kevin's turn to take a step back and consider all that had been said. The confrontation hadn't eased Mark's discomfort any, because Kevin might be too bitter and angry to ever change his ways. But Mark left the condo feeling like he had won a bit of vindication for both himself and Jennifer.

# Eleven

A week passed quickly, and the Bulls moved onward, to the finals, following a grueling, semi-finals victory over the Detroit Pistons. Animosity always ruled when the Bulls and Pistons faced off, and Chicago's team had been stretched to the limit during this trip down the hardcourts, winning the series four games to three.

Currently processing a sidebar on the semi's, Jennifer didn't pay much mind to her neighbor in the next cubical, Samantha Malone, until she said admiringly, "Used to be I thought all the good men in this world were married."

The words stopped Jennifer cold, for Samantha was looking directly at Mark.

"What's that?" Jennifer asked, assuming a nonchalant air.

"I find it hard to believe a man like Mark Abington is single and unattached. I think he's incredible."

*Join the club,* Jennifer thought tartly, trying her best not to scowl or give herself away. "Well, he's single, but he does date frequently."

Samantha leaned closer and gave her a conspiratory look. Jennifer felt guilty. This woman thought she was sharing a confidence with someone who was impartial.

"I've done some checking, shameless woman that I am, and found out he's not dating anyone *seriously.*" She shrugged happily. "In that case, as far as I'm concerned, all's fair."

Jennifer kept quiet.

"I've been divorced for nearly a year," Sam continued, "and I've been leery of getting involved again for Joshua's sake. It's bad enough if I get hurt, I don't want him getting hurt, too." She stretched her legs out, giving Jennifer a steady look. "Mark is different, though. Something about the man just sets a person at ease. He's trustable."

Bring a kid into the picture and I turn into a marshmallow, Jennifer thought, distracting herself by focusing on her wire copy and computer terminal. "I don't blame you for being cautious. I think that's smart."

"I hear you're good friends with Mark. Is that right?"

"The best," Jennifer answered with emphasis. "Why?" With clarity Jennifer now understood why people could be driven to violence over jealousy and deep feelings toward another person. She felt like throttling Samantha for even looking at Mark, let alone entertaining thoughts of starting a relationship with him.

And the last thing she wanted to do was answer a litany of questions about Mark.

Nevertheless, Jennifer wanted to know what she was up against. Cut right to it, she thought, and find out what's on Samantha's mind, because if she could, this woman would be with Mark in a minute.

"I give you a lot of credit. I don't think I could just be friends with a man like Mark. He's got too much sex appeal. Too much charisma. I'd be a goner in a minute. He's gorgeous."

Astute comment, Jennifer thought. Nowadays she found herself wondering how they had ever existed on friendship alone. As lovers they shared so much more—yet risked so much more as a result.

"True," Jennifer answered after a time, sounding as hesitant as she felt. How was she supposed to handle this? "He's a terrific man. I consider myself lucky." She tried to figure out what else to say without giving away too much. "You're interested in Mark, huh?"

Wistfully, a smile crossing her face, Samantha nodded. "You bet." Quickly her eyes returned to Jennifer, and she warned, "But that's between you, me, and the desktop, Jen. Okay?"

Hoping her face looked impassive, Jennifer answered, "Promise, Sam."

But on the inside, her blood pumped with an onslaught of panic inspired energy.

"Hey Jen!" In passing, Kylie got no answer to her greeting, so she paused, focusing on her friend. "Why so melancholy?"

"Have you got a minute? In private?"

"For you, always."

There was no need to discuss logistics. Retrieving their purses, they went to the women's lavatory.

"What's up?" Kylie asked, once they were certain of being alone. "You're wound up like a watch." She laughed with good spirit. "You nervous about the company softball game tonight? I noticed you bet an entire five dollars on the *Tribe* in this week's pool. You must have been on sinus medication."

Jennifer laughed, too. "No, I placed a heavy bet on the *Tribe* because we're playing Kevin's radio station. He'll be there. I took great satisfaction in betting against him, despite the daunting odds."

"So what's going on?"

Jennifer leaned against a porcelain sink. "I want an honest answer about something."

"Sure."

"If you were Mark . . ."

"Ha!" Kylie interrupted with a smirk. "If I were Mark, I'd be with *Sports Illustrated,* in New York, living the good life."

"You brat! Get serious. I've got a problem."

"Okay. Sorry. If I were Mark?"

"If you were Mark, would you be attracted to someone like Samantha?"

Kylie's brows rose, and her eyes widened. "Are you still keeping tabs on those two?"

Jennifer didn't share her friend's light hearted mood. "I just had a very informative conversation with Samantha. In no uncertain terms, she just told me she's interested in Mark. Couldn't be more delighted that he's unattached. She's amazed I'm *just friends* with him because he's so sexy."

A wince came as Kylie's answer. "Oh, Jen. Did she actually *say* this?"

"Yes! I promised her I wouldn't say anything, but Kylie, you're the only one who knows about Mark and myself. I had to tell you or go nuts worrying. She's after him and doesn't even realize my feelings, or his. What am I supposed to do?"

"Tell Mark."

She seemed definitive on the matter, but Jennifer couldn't quite see why. "Tell Mark that a vivacious, beautiful woman is interested in him? Kylie, are you out of your mind?"

"No. I'm giving you sound advice. Look, Jen, you've got two options the way I see it. You either tell him, or tolerate the fact that she'll be after him and have faith in Mark. Regardless, I don't think he'll let you down. He's in love with you."

"Funny, I remember having that same kind of confidence in Kevin once." Kylie gave her a frustrated look. "Sam will be at the game tonight. I'm curious to see what she's like after working hours. I wonder if she'll . . ."

"Jump his bones?" Kylie offered in her typically irreverent manner. They shared a hearty laugh, and not for the first time, Jennifer started to feel stupid about her overblown reactions to Samantha Malone.

Kylie continued. "If it'll make you feel better to have him savvy about what's going on, then tell him Sam's interested. Otherwise, you're going to have to have some trust. I know how tough that would be for you, though."

Jennifer shook her head, absently studying the drab-looking wall across from her. "I told Sam I wouldn't say anything, and my word should count for something, so I won't tell Mark. That would be hurtful. But if she makes a move on him, I'll lose it, Kylie. After the way Kevin dumped me, this is seeming too much like déjà-vous for my comfort."

"In that case, you'll have to play it by heart." Kylie gripped her arm and gave it a shake. "Trust your instincts."

"Then I've got to keep quiet. I promised her. Besides, I have to learn to have faith in Mark."

That was hard for her to say, though, considering the past. After all, how could she justify being so faithless? Mark had never given her cause to doubt him. In over two years, he had been her soul-mate. She had found the perfect man, and he had been part of her life for years. Why couldn't she simply forget the Gwynn Aldridge's and Samantha Malone's of this world and simply love him?

Because she had put all of her trust in a man she had loved enough to agree to marry.

Her trust had been rewarded with pain—the kind of deep, stinging pain that alters a person's heart forever. And on one level, Jennifer had enormous faith in Mark. He was a wonderful man who deserved that latitude. But Samantha clouded her rational line of thinking.

Before she and Kylie left the restroom, Jennifer looked at her friend and made a resounding declaration—despite the doubts and fears. "Mark and I belong together. Nothing, and no one, will change that fact."

* * *

Hot, dry air kicked up dirt from the baseball diamond, sending dust into a swirl. *Home Run Haven,* a massive plot of land that hosted six separate baseball fields, hummed with activity since each of the diamonds was currently in use.

Of most interest to the general public was the charity sponsored, media softball game being played between WCIO Radio and the *Sentinel* on diamond number five.

Sitting on a bench with the rest of her team, Jennifer scanned the bleachers surrounding their baseball diamond. They were packed, but she found the person she looked for with ease.

Brenda Sheffield. Cheering for Kevin. Jennifer felt like squirming with disgust, or at the very least, muttering a few choice obscenities about the woman. Even wearing a tee-shirt that bore Kevin's morning show insignia and plain-styled shorts, Brenda managed to look chic, somehow above the crowd. Perhaps it was the perfect fall of her thick, red hair, or her flawless, fair complexion.

*Déjà-vous.* Her glance skimmed to Samantha, who sat not far away. Samantha was dressed identical to Jennifer, in a team uniform of gold, blue, and white. To Jennifer, though, Samantha seemed crisper, more energetic. *But, in truth, was she?*

"Need a confidence implant?" Kylie whispered, sitting down on the bench next to Jennifer. She had noticed the direction of Jennifer's gaze.

She grinned. "Do doctors perform those now? If so, I might be interested."

Kylie gave her a nudge, looking toward the entrance gate. "Why look, here comes just what you need . . ."

Mark walked through an opening in the chain link fence that surrounded their playing field. Giving high-fives to several of his teammates, he tossed off jokes and smiles, sliding off his sunglasses when he neared the team dugout.

Jennifer sighed at the sight of him. "Never has a baseball uniform had it so good."

They shared a laugh until Mark snapped a towel near their legs. "Break it up you two or you're headed for the showers." He snickered. "With me, of course, your devoted starting pitcher."

"In your dreams, Abington," Jennifer razed. She gave his shoulder a playful shove when he sat down next to her.

No sooner had the dust settled around Mark's cleats than Samantha breezed by, wicked smile and all. She maneuvered her way into the teasing spell, peeking over the edge of her shades as she took to the field. "Mmmmm . . . great set of . . . *legs,* Abington."

"Malone, you're insubordinate! Get your butt to right field," he assigned with gleeful maliciousness. "Out where the weeds grow!"

Chuckling at the way he had put Samantha in her place, Jennifer doubled over and slid her leather baseball glove from beneath the bench. The others stood and assembled on the field en masse.

As she was hunched over, a pair of feet came to a stop directly in front of her. "Hey, Jen."

Her movements froze for a moment when she recognized Kevin's voice.

"Fraternizing with the enemy?" she questioned with deceptive lightness, refusing to look up until she was good and ready.

"Perhaps."

Rising slowly, she looked up a distance, into his surprisingly complacent face. Personally, especially after his support at the funeral, Jennifer had no beef with him, but he had been treating Mark horribly.

"What do you want?"

He extended a hand. "To wish you luck." Baffled, Jennifer didn't readily accept the gesture. Kevin clucked his tongue when his hand remained suspended, its call unanswered. "I also wanted to say hello to you. Any crime in that? I haven't seen you in a while, and I wanted to make sure you're doing okay."

Still skeptical, Jennifer stood. "I'm fine, Kevin. Don't worry about me." She nodded toward the bleachers, in Brenda's general direction. "You've got enough on your plate already."

Kevin didn't accept that comment with a tolerant scowl or an equally cutting reply as expected. He remained impassive but his eyes clouded, seeming sad. "You're right, Jen," he answered instead. "It seems I got more than I bargained for when I left you."

He started to walk away, but Jennifer caught up and matched his stride, following him toward WCIO's dugout. "What's that supposed to mean? What's wrong?"

Kevin turned, issuing a stern reprimand. "Never mind. Forget it, Jen. I don't think I can mend fences. It's too late. Get to the field, sweetheart. There's liable to be fireworks if you're seen in enemy territory."

And he didn't mean the WCIO dugout. He was looking at Mark. Something was on Kevin's mind, something that made him decidedly uncomfortable.

"Are you going to *Duggan's Pub* after the game?" she asked.

"Why?"

"If you are, we could talk. We're not a couple anymore, Kevin, but there's no reason why I can't be a friend if you're feeling down about something. After all, you've been there for me."

He touched her face, looking once more toward the pitching mound where Mark stood. Quickly he dropped his arm to his side. "No can do, Jen. Brenda and I have some things to hash out so we're planning on an early night."

Subtle though it was, Jennifer had noticed the way Kevin reacted to Mark. "Stop looking at Mark and look at me. Don't worry about him. If you need to talk, we'll talk."

Again Kevin responded in the negative, shaking his head. "He was right you know."

Kevin looked so deeply into her eyes, Jennifer could feel his intensity, sense his embattled spirit. "Right about what?"

"Mark once said I miss what I've lost." Regretfully he shook his head. "I can't get you back, Jen. I know that now. Still, I miss you. Guess I might be learning from my mistakes after all."

Jennifer spared a glance toward Brenda, not admiring her or envying her the way she had scant moments ago. "Regardless, I hope everything works out for you, Kevin. You may not believe this, but I want the best for you."

"I believe you, Jen. That's a classy thing to say, and you've always been a classy lady."


"Eh, Brewer," a disgruntled colleague spoke up, "be thankful the *Sentinel* softball team is a lot better at covering sports than covering a point-spread. The employee betting pool lost a bundle today. We got pasted!"

Tom Brewer protested that line of thinking, lifting his mug of frosty cold beer in salute. "Well, our team may have lost, but I've never seen such graceful strike-outs as those perpetrated by *Tribe* newcomer Samantha Malone."

The assemblage gathered at *Duggan's Pub* lifted their glasses as well, a chorus of "Here, here!" filling the air.

Sitting next to Mark, Jennifer watched Samantha blush and look embarrassed as she pinned a slice of hair behind her ear.

"My goodness," Samantha cooed, "such adulation! I feel like I fit right in here."

Mark whooped. "Yeah, Sammie, none of us can play worth a damn either. Welcome to *The Sentinel Tribe.*"

Laughing they clinked glasses across the table and she rolled her eyes. "Oh, my plaque please! A trophy perhaps?" With a devilish expression, she turned to Tom Brewer, "I know . . . a page-long write up in tomorrow's edition?"

Groaning, Tom poised his beer mug over her head, threatening to pour the dark amber liquid. "If you dare to make another outrageous demand . . ."

"Uncle! Uncle! I surrender!" Laughing even harder, along with everyone else at the table, Samantha's flirtatious gaze strayed to Mark.

Jennifer's levity was conspicuously missing. She sat silently, feeling the dank, smoke fetid air close in around her. Increasingly uncomfortable, she listened to the jokes and laughter that revolved around Samantha, yet didn't feel like a part of the raucous crowd.

Mark sensed her ill vibes. He had felt them before, in Toronto, when she had been troubled about his job offer from *Sports Illustrated,* and again when Gwynn had shown up unexpectedly. Something was eating at her nerves tonight and he wanted to soothe her.

Shifting his body, he inched closer to her, slipping his hand across her knees. Gently, he caressed her thigh beneath the table.

Their eyes met and held. Jennifer smiled, discreetly, for him alone, mouthing the words, *"Thank you."*

A high-spirited dance number signaled the start to a night of dancing at the bar and Samantha stood immediately, calling, "Abington, let's see if you're better at dancing than you are at pitching."

Anger boiled beneath Jennifer's skin. *Damn her for being so free-spirited and fun. And while we're at it, damn her feelings for the man I love!*

Mark had no choice, she knew. To refuse such a seemingly innocent request would be uncalled for. Flicking Jennifer a brief, apologetic look, he moved away. She shrugged, feeling cold as his possessive caress strayed from her thigh.

Standing, he gave Samantha a warm smile. "Okay, strike-out queen, you've got it."

On the dance floor, Mark and Samantha moved amidst a pack of people. Music blasted from the gigantic speakers, the beat fast and furious. For that entire four minute stretch, he felt awful about being with Samantha and not Jennifer.

When the song concluded, he took Samantha's arm immediately. Leading her toward an alcove, he decided to forego the potential consequences and tell her about his relationship with Jennifer. Otherwise, it seemed danger would lurk. Besides, he wasn't so sure anymore if silence and protectiveness would serve their relationship best. Briefly he scanned the secluded, corner table where the *Sentinel* employees sat, seeking Jennifer's face.

He dropped his hold on Samantha, already moving away as he murmured, "Just a second, Sammie. I need to check on something."

Jennifer's spot at the table was empty.

*Brenda, Brenda, Brenda.* Jennifer couldn't help thinking that Samantha was just like her.

*But* she had to ask herself, and not for the first time, *is Mark like Kevin?*

In the ladies restroom, she stared at her reflection in the mirror, trying to compose herself against the fierce bite of jealousy she felt.

*Meyers,* she chastised herself, *sulking and being hurt isn't going to do you any good—not against a natural-born charmer like Samantha Malone.*

But how could she compete? Her relationship with Kevin had taught her clearly that she didn't have the killer instinct for doing battle over the love of a man.

For now, all she wanted to do was go home. Thoughts of escape seduced her like the proverbial serpent.

"Jennifer, are you all right?"

She sighed silently at the sound of Samantha's voice, thinking, *Lord, this just isn't my night.* "I'm fine, Sam. I needed a breather, that's all."

"Oh." Samantha looked angry, and as she touched up her lipstick and ran a comb through her hair, her eyes kept zeroing in on Jennifer. Finally she reported coolly, "Mark is concerned about you. He's waiting outside."

*Damn! Leave it alone, Samantha,* she felt like saying. Jennifer didn't keep her bitterness in check. "Yeah? So what if he is?"

She shook her head. "He's awfully possessive about you."

Through tightly clenched teeth, Jennifer hissed, "Yes he is, Sam. Why is that a problem?"

"You need to ask? Jen, I told you how I felt, but you know what I've figured out? You never told me how you feel about Mark."

Glaring hotly, Jennifer replied, "That's none of your business."

She started to walk away, but Samantha caught her arm. "Okay, you've just put me in my place, Jennifer. But understand this—you've got no more hold over him than I do. You're not engaged to him, or married. I like him a lot, and Mark Abington is fair game. I have as much a chance with him as you do. Keep that in mind."

No words could have made her feel more sick. With startling efficiency, Samantha had just taken a scalpel to Jennifer's most vulnerable spot.

"I had a feeling your friendship theme with him was nothing more than a sham."

Jennifer didn't wait around to hear more. Leaving the bathroom, she ran almost directly into Mark.

"Come on. We're leaving," he ordered.

He had already collected her softball jacket. Without waiting for an answer he grabbed her hand and they left *Duggan's Pub.*

Stony silence accompanied them to her apartment. Mark drove, glowering at the road ahead, his emotions simmering.

"Jennifer, I didn't do anything wrong!" he finally said. "I didn't seduce the woman! Hell, I'm not even attracted to her! Don't you see that?"

"Lay off, Mark."

"No! I'm not avoiding this anymore." Stopped beneath the glow of a red light, Mark turned to her. "I'm sick of this! You've been sulking about Sam since the day she hired on. And as far as tonight goes, I seem to remember in Toronto you said you enjoyed the outgoing side of my personality. You even said you envied it."

"Amongst a crowd!" she stormed. *"Not* with other women."

On a groan, Mark gave up the fight, not wanting to argue with her while operating a piece of heavy machinery.

Part of him felt glad she was so jealous. There was something appealing about her show of possessiveness. What kept hitting home of late, though, was how deeply Kevin's affair with Brenda had eroded her self-confidence and ego.

At her apartment, almost instantly after closing the door behind them, Mark turned the tables on her.

"You're afraid of me leaving you for another woman, like Kevin did. Am I right?"

Sullen, she nodded.

"Let me ask you something, Face. Who's to say someday you won't meet a man and end up saying, 'Gee, if only I weren't involved with Mark.' "

"Easy," she interrupted firmly. "There are two very specific reasons why that won't happen."

"Name them."

"Number one, *I've been there*. That's the way I got my heart broken and I know how that kind of betrayal feels. Never would I subject someone to that kind of pain. That's why I have to be so sure of how committed we are to each other."

"And number two?"

"Number two," she answered tentatively, "is that I love you, too much to even *think* about another man, let alone develop a relationship with someone else."

Mark smiled, thinking, *checkmate sweetheart*. "Right back at you, Face."

She pinned her lower lip with her teeth, thinking of how undeniably sincere he sounded. "Lately I've been so jealous—I've felt so spiteful, that I don't even feel worthy of you, Mark."

"Then you need to be assured of the fact that you belong to me. Don't you see? You're part of my heart, part of my well-being. Without you I'm so much less. You fulfill me. How can anyone, or anything come between that?"

"But Samantha . . . women like her . . . intimidate me." Emotionally unsteady, she paced through the space of her living room. "They didn't used to. I used to be one of the care-free, party loving people of the world. Now, I look at her and I see everything I'm not."

The only way to win this argument, Mark knew, would be to take her self-doubts and smash them. One by one.

"How does she intimidate you?" He felt glad to see that she paused, struggling for a moment to find an adequate response.

"Well . . . off hand, I'd say she's more appealing. More spunky."

"You're equally as vibrant, but in a different way."

"What?"

"Samantha Malone may be gregarious and have a lot of gusto, but she doesn't have your tenderness. She's not as innately sweet as you are." He stroked her cheek. "She'd never be anyone's secret admirer."

"You're mocking me!"

"No I'm not!" It grated him that she refused to see his point. "Damn it, Jen, *you* appeal to me. You. She'll never be my buddy. She'll never know the history that you and I have shared. Be secure in my feelings for you. We're so lucky, Face. We're not just lovers, we're friends."

"Then you care about my feelings?"

"Ridiculous question."

"Then stay away from her, Mark. Keep clear of Samantha Malone. She's very interested in you, and because of the fact that we're being private about our relationship, she thinks she has a chance to be with you. I'm telling you, she'll stir up trouble."

Not one word had gotten through to her. Mark's eyes narrowed and he clenched his jaw. "Trouble for who, Jennifer. Me or you?"

Brushing past him, haughty, proud and hurt, Jennifer opened the door. "Obviously you're not willing to understand, or do as I've asked. Good-night, Mark."

But he didn't leave yet. Roughly he pulled her close, the conquest of his mouth overshadowing her exclamation of surprise. Pinning her against the wall, he slammed the door shut and pressed into her, hard and demanding.

She fought against him, trying to push him back, but he captured her hands and forced them to the wall next to her head. The whole time their bodies crushed together, greedy for pleasure, on fire with passion they both knew would go unfulfilled.

That didn't stop the torture of his kiss, though, the smooth, warm invasion of his hands into her hair, forcing her to be still while he conquered her will and her body with an effectiveness that left her reeling.

Finally he pulled back, throbbing with desire, needing her love so desperately. "I won't accept an ultimatum. So you take that kiss to bed with you tonight, Face, along with the heat and the longing.

See if being away from me brings you the sanctuary you're looking for. My bet is it won't. For either one of us."

"Mark, how about lunch today? Are you free? We need to set up an itinerary for the trip to Los Angeles."

If a person could win awards for poor timing, Jennifer thought, Samantha Malone would be champ—hands down.

Sitting across from Mark, discussing a Sunday magazine spread they were putting together on Chicago Bears coach Dave Wannstedt, Jennifer's body went stiff.

"I'd love to, Sammie," he answered, "but I've got a feature I need to put to bed before we leave. Jen and I are working on it now."

Tension ran so thick, sparks could have ignited in the small space of Mark's office.

"Fine, but the travel agent wants our reservations and you gave them *my* name. They're on my hide." With a soft, cajoling smile, she offered, "Just give me lunch. Jen can have you the rest of the day."

She was deliberately pushing, Jennifer knew. They'd discuss plans, to be sure, but only in a superficial way. The deeper meaning behind this lunch date was the fact that Samantha wanted time alone with Mark.

*Trust him,* her heart instructed. *So be it,* her head answered. And Jennifer decided to give Samantha Malone a lesson in grace.

Uncrossing her legs with an indulgent smile to them both, Jennifer stood and looked straight into Mark's eyes. "Do lunch, buddy. She's insisting." Gathering up her papers and a cassette recorder, she said further, "There's no pressure on my part. When you get back, we'll finish the story on Wannstedt."

Her reward was one heck of a smile, full of knowing, full of love. "Thanks, Face."

It felt good, she decided, to have faith. "No problem."

Smoothly she turned, giving Samantha a brief nod. "Excuse me."

She watched them leave, saw Samantha toss her head and laugh at something Mark said. A sharp twinge of jealousy poked her nerves, but Jennifer knew she had to temper that emotion or end up losing Mark. *Faith,* she kept reiterating to herself, *keep faith in him. He deserves that much.*

Consulting her daily assignment list, she gathered wire reports and started to write the *Sports Round-Up* section of the *Sentinel* which entailed capsuling national sports stories and molding them into a half page run down.

But that task ran a distant second to the pattern of her thoughts.

*I let Kevin leave without a backward glance once Brenda invaded his heart. I didn't have the confidence in myself to do battle with her. Maybe my feelings weren't strong enough for him. But not this time. If Samantha is after Mark, I'll fight her tooth and nail. I won't be left out in the cold again. I only hope Mark is immune to her charms because I love him beyond reason. I can't stand the thought of another woman sharing with him the things I do.*

*I won't let him go without a war.*

# Twelve

Jennifer swayed in Mark's arms and couldn't help smiling. "You consider this being discreet about our relationship?"

Slow dancing with Mark, Jennifer felt like her feelings were as transparent as glass. Frankly, as he held her close and looked into her eyes, she could have cared less.

"I sure do."

An early summer breeze lifted off the white-capped waves of Lake Michigan, blowing cool and fresh. Tonight was a *Sentinel* tradition, a "Finals Frenzy" party, hosted by Tom Brewer at his northshore home in Highland Park.

"I've often wondered, what happens if the Bulls don't make the finals?" Jennifer said. "Over the past few years, this has become a great party."

Mark laughed, the sound low and seductive. "There's always an excuse for a party, Face. Always."

Employees and family members of the *Sentinel* sports department were in full attendance at the bash, nearly 40 in all, and Tom had already overseen a barbecue of hamburgers and hotdogs.

Now, as people mingled together and danced, Jennifer and Mark enjoyed the relaxation of celebrating with friends. They had been together exclusively, sometimes sitting at linen covered tables with colleagues, other times sitting quietly to enjoy the music being piped outdoors from the stereo, or joining in the dancing from time to time.

If anyone took note of them being together, it wouldn't have appeared too unusual, Jennifer figured, since they had often attended parties together. Apparently they could fool everyone—with a solitary, notable exception. Samantha Malone.

On Monday morning, Mark would be leaving for Los Angeles

and Jennifer still dreaded the prospect of a separation. Especially since he would be with Samantha almost constantly. But her trust index had begun to rise and assure.

"I know what you're thinking about," he chastised gently, still guiding her in a dance.

"Don't be so smart," she retorted. "You just might be wrong."

"Nope. Not this time. A storm cloud named Malone just darkened those otherwise lovely features of yours, Face."

He emphasized the word *Face* to bring his point home and the joking tone he used made her smile, despite the truth behind his observation.

He gave a low laugh. "Know what?" Jennifer shook her head and leaned back to meet his eyes. "I think Jason has given up on you. That should make you happy, especially since he seems quite taken with Sam. He's been keeping her busy most of the night. So don't be glum, she's stayed out of our way."

"Out of *your* way," Jennifer clarified. "Me she could care less about." Beneath her hand, Jennifer felt his shoulders shake with repressed laughter. She gave Mark a blank look. "What's so funny?"

Looking over Jennifer's shoulder, he spied Samantha and Jason dancing together. "I don't know where this idea came from, but I was just thinking we should introduce her to Kevin."

Jennifer hooted. "They'd shoot off some fireworks together."

Mark shifted against her and ended their dance. He maneuvered her toward the dock, where Tom's cabin cruiser bobbed in the water. Cutting across the perfectly tended lawn, he walked Jennifer to the boat slip so they could have some privacy. In unison they sat down on the dock.

Rolling up her slacks, Jennifer made a happy exclamation and kicked off her espadrilles so she could dangle her feet in the water.

"Speaking of Kevin . . ." Mark began.

Coquettishly, Jennifer replied, "Were we speaking of Kevin?"

"Yes we were. A while ago. Pay attention, dear."

"Ummm."

"Kevin and I had a . . . well . . . discussion I haven't told you about yet."

"Oh?" She sloshed her feet happily, the bracing water invigorating her skin. She thought of the baseball game, and how strangely Kevin had acted then. With an inquiring expression she asked, "What did you two *discuss?*"

"His method of operations regarding his friends."

"You're kidding."

"Nope. No joke. After our confrontation about Sam, I got mad enough to rake him over the coals about what he's done to you, and to me, and what he'll probably end up doing to Brenda once he gets bored with her. He's a good guy, Jen, but he needs to . . ."

"Learn from past mistakes?" she offered in an absent way, still watching him carefully. She recalled those very words from Kevin, and how depressed he had been.

"Past mistakes exactly. He knocked you for a loop and he climbed all over me for no good reason and I've been his closest friend for almost fifteen years."

"I'm glad you got through to him."

Mark smirked. "I didn't say I got through to him. Actually, he called me a sanctimonious jerk and basically told me where to go with my self-righteous ideas. But maybe there's hope. Since then we're getting along a lot better."

Silence fell between them.

"Speaking of past alliances," he continued with a grin.

Jennifer giggled. "Were we speaking of past alliances?"

"Face, pay attention, please." Gently, he bumped his shoulder against hers. Undeterred he asked, "Remember about a year ago, when you moved?"

Mark's question came out of the blue and took her by surprise. "Sure. You helped me. Are you still waiting for a thank you note?"

"Um-hum." He sidled her a glance, his lips twitching. "C'mon. Do you *remember?*"

After an uncomfortable pause, Jennifer replied, "Okay, okay. I remember being mad at you."

Mark nodded, and waited. Removing his socks and shoes, he dipped his feet, too. "Do you remember why you were mad?"

Jennifer scowled at him, though with good humor. "Is there any particular reason why you're taunting me like this, Abington?"

Indulgent to no end, Mark requested, "Bear with me."

"Tolerance *is* a virtue." She looked out, across the line of pale water that stretched endlessly before them, her emotions tangling up. "I was mad at you about Gwynn. I remember that distinctly."

"Yes, because she had been cutting in on the amount of time you and I could spend together."

Jennifer cringed. "I was so terrible." Water rushed to the shore, ebbing and flowing as waves tumbled over one another. A light, tangy scent rose from the water, mixing with the aroma of the leaves, the freshly mown grass.

She went on. "You had very kindly offered to help me move. It was a Saturday. Then, the night before hand, Gwynn got a hold of some theatre tickets and wanted you to go. You said you could still help me move, but not for as long." She shook her head. "I blew up. Read you the riot act. Gwynn had usurped me, and I hated not being able to share things with you like we had before; or have the access to you that I had before." Nostalgic, she grinned, still looking out across the lake. "I yelled at you about friendship being as much of a commitment, at times, as a marriage. You had to work at it or it would die." Her gaze swung to Mark. "I felt useless to you."

"After that argument," Mark supplied, "you all but dared me to show up the next day and help you move. Defied me to be of any help to you at all. What were your exact words . . . ? Oh yeah—I remember. You said, 'I don't need you, but "Lady Gwynneth of Cling Wrap" does, so go to her.' "

Apologetic, she gave Mark a wide eyed look. "In my own defense, Marcus Allen, you have to give me credit for becoming friends with her. I liked Gwynn, but at that point, I felt useless. I wonder if insecurity is a genetic trait for me."

He moved a bit closer, but didn't dare put an arm around her, or draw her face to his, like he wanted to. That would have called attention to them. "I give you a lot of credit for being a friend to Gwynn, but remember, I showed up the next day. I understood how you felt."

She smiled at the memory. Naturally, following the dictates of Murphy's Law, the day had been rainy and cold. Mark had arrived dripping with water, carrying a bag of fresh donuts and two styrofoam cups of coffee. They hadn't said a word by way of greeting. He had simply moved past her, dived into their breakfast and, after that, went to work loading and unloading her belongings.

"I remember all this, Mark, but I still don't get your point."

"Count on me." Their eyes made a connection between their hearts. "Reward my love and my loyalty with trust, Face. Okay?"

"I'll try," she answered softly.

He couldn't resist snuggling a bit closer, though he still kept their physical contact at a minimum. "I didn't rush off that night to be with Gwynn. I had turned down her invitation. So, that night, you and I stayed together after dinner and talked for hours while we sat on the floor in your living room and played backgammon."

"That meant a lot to me."

"I know, and I know how hard the week to come will be for you. But when I come home from L.A., with my conscience intact and my trustability affirmed, I expect you to give me one hell of a welcome party."

"Got a guest list made up?" she asked huskily.

"There's only one name on it. Yours." Pondering the discussion they had just had, Mark added, "You know, when I look at things now, I'd say you and I were laying the ground work even then. You were jealous, and I cared more about your feelings than Gwynn's."

Jennifer was startled by that piece of insight. "You're probably right. I never thought of it that way before now."

"Me either." Beneath the water, he slid his cool, bare feet against hers, which made them both smile like kids with a secret. "I'll miss you."

"You better."

Mark laughed at the stern look on her face. "Promise."

Just as quickly, her face softened into loving, vulnerable lines. "I'll miss you too, Mark."

Playful, he tickled the bottom of her foot with his big toe. "You better."


After Tom's party, Mark took Jennifer home and the glow of the evening refused to fade.

"Strange, isn't it?"

"What?" Next to him in the car, Jennifer enjoyed the view of his vivid, masculine profile. He took her hand and brought it to rest against his leg.

"Do you realize this is technically one of our first dates?"

Her love rose up, and she watched him with fascination. "Well in that case, let me tell you what a wonderful time I had, Mr. Abington." Blowing very softly into his ear, nipping at it with tender bites, she murmured, "But, since this is a first date and all, you might have to leave me on the doorstep with a chaste peck on the cheek."

Never taking his eyes from the road, his lips curving in a way that made desire simmer in the air, Mark growled, "Like hell I will."

And he made good on that vow.

At her apartment, Mark closed the door behind them, that soft, final click reverberating through the air. Jennifer's breath caught. Never had a man looked at her with such unbridled intensity. Taut and heady, his tension stretched forward, wrapping her in heat and promise.

Raw need burned in his eyes, but this, she knew, was an incredibly sensual man. Passion held sway, but Mark knew instinctively how to rein in control and give his feelings away as freely as he accepted what was given to him.

As only the best of lovers can do.

A tremor worked through her, alerting her senses of what was to come, her body opening, aching to receive, to give . . .

Mark stepped close, slow and deliberate. When he stood only centimeters away, he reached up, silently drawing a line from her chin down her throat. Against the thin, cotton fabric of her shirt, his fingertip trailed between her breasts. In response, her nipples came to life, peaking against the material.

A tiny sound of pleasure escaped her lips. Jennifer took his hands, placing them on her hips then sliding them up, across her mid-section, her ribcage. When his fingers made contact with the underside of her breasts, Jennifer's lower body pressed forward automatically, seeking him on much deeper levels.

But he moved away, a mystical, sexy glint enlivening his eyes. "Come with me, to your bedroom, Jen."

His voice was heavy with passion, gravelly.

Thick and molten, a delicious throb began to pound at the juncture of her legs, stirring restlessness.

Answering the call of sensuousness, she took his hands, leading him down the hallway.

Deep inside, desperation seemed to fuel Mark's mood and actions. This show of intensity caught Jennifer off guard, frightened her a bit, yet excited her at the same time.

"Sit down," she beckoned softly, directing him to the bed. She turned on a light. "You were the instigator last time. Let me have a turn."

She made her humble request, but awaited an answer before proceeding. Bewitched already, Mark nodded, settling lengthwise on the comforter of her bed.

A hush settled over the room, stilling all but her shallow breaths, all but the blood searing through his veins. Mark waited, anticipated, feeling on fire for her already. His imagination took flight . . .

Jennifer began by freeing her hair from its loosely fashioned ponytail. Reassembling the waves with her fingers, her eyes remained steadily on Mark.

Pulling away the loose fitting, pastel tee-shirt she wore, Jennifer stood before him, proud and alluring, a seduction of peaches and creme. She unfastened her shorts and let them fall to the floor so she could step them aside.

Affected, Mark moved restlessly on her bed. Desire and heat sifted together to harden his body, yet soften his soul.

Her underclothes were of powder-blue silk, tiny slips of gossamer cover that didn't as much hide as entice. Thin straps of silk curved around her hips, plunging between her legs, toward the center of her, in a V of satin that Mark longed to caress and explore. He felt his body react, his manhood beneath the loose linen of his shorts twitching with eager vitality.

Eye to eye with him, she reached up, to the shadowy cleft between her breasts and unfastened her bra, letting it, too, fall unheeded to the carpeting at her feet.

Mark could take no more. He stood, before she could speak a word, joining her, caressing her warm, pliant skin.

Cupping first one breast, then the other, he molded her flesh then bent his head low on a moan of pleasure, nuzzling the soft mounds. She smelled like flowers after a hot, summer rain.

He touched each pebbled tip with his tongue, at first to tease, then to salve them with long, strident swipes. He groaned, knowing he was dangerously close to losing control. Her body arched against him, sliding against his shaft, and the sound of her soft whimper made him shiver.

And he hadn't really done a thing. Yet.

"Let me, Jen." He finished off her harem-girl seduction, bringing her hands to rest on his shoulders. "You stay put . . ."

And he moved away, just inches. Kneeling, he slid his flattened hand down her tummy, across the swatch of silk, cupping her intimately as he continued the caress, slowly, touching the opening of her body. He came immediately upon her dampness.

Clutching his shoulders convulsively, Jennifer surrendered, opening her legs, moving into a more accommodating position. "Mark . . ."

"Relax, Face. Let me do this . . . let me give this to you . . ."

He looked into her eyes briefly, searching for approval, and wasn't denied.

As he caressed her inner thigh, he felt a tremor glide down her body. She was holding herself in tight check, not quite knowing what to expect, but she was also wet and warm, ready for his touch, for his love.

Mark pulled her panties away and Jennifer felt her knees threaten to give way as he tasted her belly button and nuzzled her abdomen with kisses. When his mouth moved lower still, she writhed toward him, pushing forward to give herself more freely. Her eyes fluttered closed when she felt his fingertips perform a gentle, rhythmic stroke, opening the tender folds of her skin, preparing her.

The touch of his lips, the careful, almost reverent way his tongue caressed that intimate opening, then slid deep, made Jennifer cry out. She clung to him tightly, fearing she'd go mad from wanting his touch, fearing she lacked the ability to hang on to this blessed insanity forever.

His loving ministrations wouldn't allow for holding back. Jennifer held fast to his shoulders, the release of her orgasm shooting ripples of ecstasy and love through her body.

As she caught her breath, Mark took her by surprise, scooping her gently into his arms. He carried her to the bed, kissing her deeply all the while, growling her name in a husky way.

Immediately he pinned her body beneath his, working free of his clothes with quick, efficient movements.

Her hand moved downward against his skin, exploring the firm ridges of his chest and stomach muscles. Glossed with sweat, Mark murmured when she reached between his legs, to caress and guide him. He welcomed the loving torment of her touch, squeezing his eyes shut as he entered her body.

Release came quickly, followed by the amazing sensation of rightness that being lovers with Jennifer had given him.

Resting against her, his breathing heavy and labored, Mark thanked fate for their friendship, and destiny for their love.

\* \* \*

The next morning, as they had done several times of late, Jennifer and Mark shared brunch on the sun kissed corner breakfast nook of her apartment. Dressed comfortably in the sleep shirt she had worn to bed, Jennifer sat down on a chrome stool next to Mark, where they shared coffee, toast, and pancakes. They spoke in hushed tones that eased them gently into the day.

When quiet spells befell them, Mark happily studied Jennifer's apartment, its healthy, leaf laden plants, the warmth of wooden end tables and plush, overstuffed furniture. He had always credited her with good taste and style. Her home, so comfortable and inviting, had always confirmed his belief. Jennifer had returned to the kitchen to cook, and replenish their plates. Delicious aromas filled the air as bacon sizzled and coffee simmered.

"I'm a lucky man," he remarked in a low voice. Their relationship still amazed him. Jennifer. His friend. His lover. The only woman he'd ever want or need in his life.

Turning from the skillet where she browned a fresh batch of pancakes, Jennifer asked, "What'd you say?"

Mark smiled, lifting his brow in an arrogant, teasing way. "Nothing, Face. Absolutely nothing."


"I'll call you from the hotel after we land."

*We.* Sitting behind her desk at work, Jennifer clenched the phone receiver tightly, hating that word with zealous passion. She had spent the entire weekend with Mark, shut off to everything in the world but him.

Now, as if Mondays weren't bad enough, the new week dawned, calling him to California and the NBA finals. *And Samantha Malone.*

Carefully she honed her voice. "I'll be waiting. Have a good trip."

"Face, it's gonna be a pain," he consoled. "Non-stop running, no sleep, crazy schedules, uncooperative athletes and coaches . . ."

He mentioned everything but Sam. She loved him all the more for that. To assure him, she teased, "You also happen to love it all, Abington, so enjoy."

His laugh reached all the way down to her stomach and made it flutter. "Yeah, guess I do. I should be hospitalized."

As the conversation progressed, Mark sounded more and more distracted. She could envision him, walking through the bedroom of his home, a wireless phone in one hand, wads of clothes in the other, an open suitcase acting as receiver to each bundle he threw. She knew Mark never packed until the day he was supposed to leave on a trip. Schedules at the *Sentinel* had a tricky way of changing at the last moment because in sports, yesterday's destination became tomorrow's aborted plan when fresh stories broke.

"Eh, Mark . . . ?"

"Yeah?" he muttered.

He was probably looking around his room, hunting for something he needed for the trip. She giggled. "Don't forget the plane tickets."

"Ha, ha, ha."

"You meeting Sam at the airport?" Sadistic question, perhaps, but Jennifer wanted to know.

"Yes. In an hour." A slight pause followed. In her mind's eye, Jennifer could see him, looking at his watch, re-checking his travel supplies. Mark's next words confirmed her assumption. "I'm late. Damn. I've gotta' go, Jen."

Firmly she nodded, that small action meant to bolster her spirits. "Have a safe flight, and a good trip. Call when you get a chance."

"Will do, Face."

". . . Bye . . ."

"I love you."

# Thirteen

"What do you mean we've been assigned to the same room?"

Mark and Samantha had just arrived at the Wyndclift Hotel in downtown Los Angeles. Following a flight full of mountain turbulence and terrible food, he had discovered a mix up in their room reservations.

Angry and tired, he stared down the hotel receptionist, waiting for an explanation.

"Listen, buddy, Los Angeles is in the midst of the NBA finals," the man justified. "Everybody who's anybody is in town, auctioning off their clothes to get a room, scalping tickets . . ."

"I could give a care," Mark answered smoothly, refusing to show his anger, or surrender the point. "My colleague and I had reserved separate suites. I don't care who's scratching for what, we have two confirmed rooms at this hotel."

"You don't understand. We received your reservation from the *Sentinel*, but we understood it was only for one room, being shared by two gentlemen, a Mark Abington and a Sam Malone."

"Give me that confirmation." Pulling a computer run-down from the hands of the clerk, Mark studied the room request.

"And obviously," Samantha retorted, "I am *not* a gentleman. *Sam* is short for Samantha."

Looking over Mark's shoulder, she pointed to the third line. "Right there, on our request form, two rooms, same floor. They botched it up, Abington."

Mark returned the print out, glowering fiercely. "Got an explanation for that, pal?"

Shaken, embarrassed, the clerk started to stammer. "Er . . . what . . . ?"

"Right there," Mark thundered, fed up with the situation. Thumping a finger against the sheet, he showed the clerk the error that had been made by the hotel. Typical trip to the Land of Fruits and Nuts, he thought wryly. "We reserved two rooms, and more importantly, we *want* two rooms."

"But sir, that's impossible. I apologize for the inconvenience, of course, but hotel space is at a premium. We're booked solid. There's no way of getting a second room at this late date. You'll have to . . ."

Wisely, the desk clerk didn't finish his thought. "Give me the damn room key," Mark demanded.

They walked away from the registration desk, hiking their luggage and carry-on bags to a corner where they could stand quietly and discuss their options.

"The way I see it, we're stuck." Mark rendered his judgment, knowing every hotel within a hundred-mile radius had more than likely been sold out for weeks.

"I can't say as I'm comfortable with the prospect of having to share quarters this week, but you're right. We don't have a choice." Blowing out a stream of air, Samantha adjusted the strap of her purse and lifted her suitcase, nodding to a bank of elevators. "Let's go."


Almost immediately after their arrival in the room, the telephone rang.

Simultaneously they turned from their open suitcases. Samantha and Mark eyed each other, silently asking the obvious.

"I'll get it." Samantha finally broke the stalemate, moving toward the phone.

Mark grabbed her arm. If the caller was Jennifer, she'd hear Samantha's voice and be furious. "No! What if it's for me? I'll get it."

That solution didn't appease Samantha in the least. "And perhaps have my son hear a man's voice when he's calling his mother's room? No way!"

The phone kept ringing.

"If it's Josh, I'll tell him the operator made a mistake. A kid would be easier to put off than anyone else."

Planting her feet, her brows furrowed, Samantha glared but didn't try to stop him. At last, on the eighth ring, Mark lifted the receiver.

"Hello?" A quick feeling of relief telegraphed through him when he heard the voice of his chief editor. "Hi, Tom. Yeah . . . just got in. The flight was fine." He rolled his eyes and Samantha smirked, at ease as well, starting to unpack again. Tom always checked in with his employees when they travelled. "Um-hum, the room is fine. Yes . . . we'll be leaving for the Forum to do preliminary interviews in about an hour. According to the schedule, that's the first media session. Okay . . . talk to you tomorrow."

After hanging up, Mark went back to unpacking, giving Samantha a quick glance. "At least the room has two full beds." She didn't answer. "Sammie?"

"Hummm?"

Still she didn't acknowledge him or give him her attention. He watched while she opened a bedside drawer, threw some belongings inside and slammed the drawer shut.

"What's the problem?"

Finally she turned, bristling with hostility. "Why didn't you tell Tom about the room snafu? I think he should know."

Smoothly he glossed over the truth. "Why bother? What good would it have done?"

"He's a chief editor at one of the nation's most influential newspapers. You don't think he'd carry a little clout? Be able to swing a favor or two?"

How could he answer that? Trouble is, he got the feeling Samantha was deliberately challenging him, wanting to force the issue—not so she could get another room, but to find out for certain what perhaps she had known all along.

Mark tried evasion once more. "Like I said, there's no need. Not even Tom could get us another room at this point."

That didn't work. He turned his back, but the action didn't deter Samantha.

"You're afraid of upsetting her, aren't you?" she asked softly. "You're afraid Jennifer will find out we've been forced to share a room."

Mark started to deny her comments, but Samantha held up a hand to quell his excuses. "Mark, you're the best writer I've ever come across, but you're a terrible actor. So is Jen. You've kept your relationship quiet, and I don't know why. It's probably none of my business, but you can be straight with me. If you're involved with her, don't lie about it. Honesty keeps the record straight. For everyone. If I'd have known, I wouldn't have hoped . . . well . . ."

The way she allowed that sentence to trail off explained a lot to Mark. No wonder Jennifer had been so jealous. *Samantha had given her cause to be.*

Pursing his lips, Mark faced her, sitting slowly on the edge of his bed. She wanted honesty, so he'd give her the flat-out, God's-honest truth. "Jennifer means more to me than any woman I've ever known. She's precious to me, and yes, we're involved. I love her very much."

Tentatively, she sat down across from him—his space, her space—yet there was no awkwardness in that distance. "Then why are you both professing to simple friendship? You've got nothing to hide."

"No we don't. At the start, for nearly two years, we were friends, Sammie. Strictly. We had a wonderful, platonic relationship. That's why Jen and I were reluctant to alter things when we found ourselves falling in love. We fought our feelings at the start, but when destiny speaks, nothing can change the result."

Wistfully she smiled. "You still didn't answer my question, Abington. Why so secretive? She told me that you two were strictly friends. She could have told the truth when I confronted her."

Mark stood, pacing the space in front of their beds. He slid his hands into the pockets of his pants and palmed some loose change, listening to the soft jingle as he spoke.

"There are a lot of reasons why we kept to ourselves, Sammie. First and foremost, we didn't want to make things uncomfortable for the people we work with. Our feelings are no one's business but our own. We didn't want well-meaning friends to butt-in and interfere. And Tom would have been concerned. He's a worrier by nature, and we didn't want to cause a needless shake-up in the sports department."

Swinging her legs, Samantha leaned back on her arms, looking at Mark with an expression of envy on her face that he found poignant.

"Then you're *with* Jennifer."

He grinned at the way she emphasized the word *with*. "Sammie, I don't remember a time now when I wasn't with her. She's my other half. She didn't lie to you about us being friends. We were, and we still are. But when we discovered love, we both realized that love is what it should have always been. No question marks, no restrictions."

Unexpectedly tears sprang to her eyes. "Oh, Mark, how I envy you."

Sitting next to her, Mark leaned on his knees so he could look into her face, which was half hidden by the fall of her hair. She didn't return his look but continued to look at the floor. "Don't envy me, Sam. Find those feelings for yourself. You will. You're fantastic."

Warily he surveyed their hotel suite, still leaning on his knees. Mark plowed his hair with his fingers and sighed, feeling uncomfortable about the entire situation.

One fact became glaringly obvious—he had to find alternate room arrangements. It had been surprising enough to discover that Jennifer's concerns about Samantha hadn't been unfounded, or jealousy inspired insecurities. He didn't want to make matters worse by spending a week beneath the same room ceiling with her.

"This isn't going to work, Sammie. You realize that, don't you?"

She gave him a blank look. "Mark, you've explained about Jennifer. There's no need to try and change rooms. I won't do anything stupid and either will you. We're adults . . ."

"True. I know we understand each other. This isn't about you and I. I'm doing this for Jennifer. I owe her that kind of reassurance. Nothing would happen between you and I, but I'll feel better knowing I've done the right thing by her—and myself.

"To be honest, hotel mix-up or not, I'd be awfully upset if roles were reversed and Jennifer were in my place. If I shared this room with you, there's no doubt that Jennifer would be furious so I'm going to check with our chief photographer and see if I can bunk with him for the week."

Samantha didn't dispute the logic of his solution. "I guess that would be more comfortable for everyone."

But Mark still felt uneasy about the potential of hurting Samantha's feelings. She had gotten caught in the middle, but he didn't want her to be pushed aside. Resting a hand on her shoulder he asked gently, "Are you sure, Sammie?"

An answer came in her sincere, though tremulous smile. Her tone of voice was endearingly acerbic. "Of course it is, Abington. Let's get to the Forum."

\* \* \*

At 9:00 the next morning, Jennifer's radio alarm went off. As usual, she had left the dial tuned to Kevin's show.

"You'll want to stay tuned in to *The Morning Line* today, folks. At the top of the hour we'll be checking in with our Sports Director, Mark Abington, who's in Los Angeles. We'll find out if Finals Weirdness has settled over the city yet. Unless you've been on Mars, you're aware of the fact that our Chicago Bulls are going for another NBA crown. Mark is on their trail and shortly we'll be giving him a surprise wake-up call to check in on pre-game hysteria."

Jennifer groaned on Mark's behalf, feeling sorry for him. Kevin and the gang would be rousing him from bed at 6 A.M. California time.

Softly she laughed, taking a portable radio with her to the bathroom so she could listen in on the program while she showered and dressed for work. "And you thought Kevin had turned more friendly. Hope you didn't have a late night, Mark."

Midway through a frothy shampoo, Jennifer cringed beneath the warm jets of water when Kevin informed his audience, "We've just put the call through to Mark's room and we're waiting for him to pick up . . . and probably start yelling . . ."

But the rich, sleep-coated voice of a woman coursed Chicago's airwaves, interrupting Kevin in mid-stride. "Hello?"

In the shower stall, Jennifer froze, soap bubbles stinging her eyes. Her arms went limp at her sides.

"Ah . . . hello . . . This is Kevin Owens from Chicago's *Morning Line*." Obviously stunned at this turn of events, Kevin asked wickedly, "I'm looking for Mark Abington."

Dead air crackled and Jennifer wiped her eyes and tossed back the ends of her hair.

"Ma . . . Mark? Who?" An irritated cluck of the tongue. "You have the wrong room. Try again."

The receiver fell into place with a loud clatter and Kevin laughed, sheepishly apologizing to the woman he had awakened.

Jennifer held no such charity.

"Damn," she cursed, slathering off the remnants of her shampoo in a vicious way. "Little do you know, Kevin. You had his room all along."

She stormed from her bathroom and went to her closet, pulling clothes from their hangers. And the woman, whose voice Jennifer knew by heart, was without question Samantha Malone.

* * *

The clamor of a ringing telephone roused Mark from a sound sleep. Mark's photographer roommate stirred, grumbled testily as he buried his head under a pillow. Mark saw all this through a muzzy haze as he lifted the receiver.

"Hello?"

"Mark, it's Samantha." And she sounded awfully hurried and alert considering the fact that the luminous dial on the clock next to his bed read the time as being 6:05 in the morning. "I just got a phone call from some radio station that's looking for you."

"Humph . . ." Mark forced his mind to function, lifting up to a sitting position while he rubbed his eyes. "Kevin? Kevin Reynolds? He called?"

"I think that was his name." She sounded shook up. "Didn't you tell the front desk you had changed rooms?"

"No, I didn't get a chance. I got so busy after going to the press conferences yesterday that I forgot about notifying the receptionist."

Then it dawned on him. *Jennifer.* She always listened to Kevin's show. She would have recognized Samantha's voice.

That thought caused panic to slosh through Mark's system and he did a large measure of waking up. "What did you say when they asked for me?"

"All I could think of to say was 'Sorry, wrong number.' A cliche I know, but it got rid of him."

"I've got to go, Sam, before he tries back."

Blindly, Mark hung up and flicked on a dim, overhead lamp so he could figure out how to dial the reception desk. He made a quick call to give them his new room number then waited, fervently praying Kevin hadn't had time to air a commercial, resume the show, and try a second call.

Minutes later, the phone rang and Mark heaved a giant sigh of relief. This had to be Kevin. He was even able to laugh when his roommate groaned and tossed in bed, swearing liberally about the sanctity of uninterrupted sleep.

Lowering his voice, hoping he sounded and acted sleepy, Mark waited several more rings then picked up the receiver. "Hello?"

Sure enough, it was Kevin. Mark growled with menace. "Kevin, you jerk, you have no respect for the concept of time zones . . ."

\* \* \*

"Ah . . . here's your *visitor,* Kevin."

The words were rife with meaning and the anticipation of Kevin's reaction. Jennifer walked into the studio, cool and defiant, casting a withering look toward the intern who had escorted her from the lobby.

"Lay off, Brian," Kevin warned, approaching Jennifer with a warm smile. "Hi, Jen."

She didn't partake in any type of preamble. "I need to talk to you, all right?"

"Sure. Let's go to my office." Once there, for additional privacy Kevin closed the door behind them. "You're ready to explode. What happened?"

Again Jennifer cut to the chase, foregoing pleasantries. "It's about your phone call to Mark this morning. Did you ask specifically for his room number or did you ask for him by name?"

"I asked for Mark by name." He shrugged. "I didn't have his room number. Why?"

She didn't answer, but spoke softly, to herself. "Then there's no way they made a mistake. If you only had his name, they would have had to look up his room number then transfer the call. This wasn't a simple case of pushing the wrong connection number. A mistake could still happen, but it wouldn't be as likely."

Kevin kept silent, listening as Jennifer spoke her thoughts aloud and paced the small quarters of his office.

"Jennifer, what are you saying? I had Mark's room all along? You think Mark had some female companionship overnight?" He paused deliberately. "And if so, does this upset you?"

"Yes it does, Kevin." She came clean about her relationship with Mark. "So you see, your assumptions about Mark and I were right on target, but we wanted to keep quiet. Then, along came Samantha Malone, a new employee at the *Sentinel. She's* the one you talked to today, the one with a voice like perfectly warmed brandy. She's turned on the charm with Mark at every opportunity, but he's been telling me I have nothing to worry about. When he left, I was ready to give him every ounce of faith and trust I have. Now she's in the room he's supposed to be at. The situation sounds awfully familiar, doesn't it?"

"Listen, Jen . . ."

Warnings sounded in his tone. He wanted to make excuses, probably for both himself and Mark. Kevin took her arm but Jennifer backed away, not wanting to hear pathetic explanations.

"No. Don't. It's the truth."

"The truth, or a reason to give up on Mark before you have the chance to get hurt again? Answer me that."

*"Both!"*

"Then let me set you straight on something, Meyers. First off, Mark wouldn't pull a stunt like that. He's too . . . too . . . *loyal.* Too mature." He gave her a look of apology. "Unlike what I did, Mark would break up with you before he betrayed you. You're his friend, Jen, you should already know this about him. God knows he's chewed me out enough times recently for listening to my hormones instead of my good sense. Well, I've started to take that advice to heart and make changes."

That caught her off guard. "What?"

"I broke up with Brenda a few days ago. She wasn't the one for me. Never was." Considering, though, he added, "Ah, but her body . . ." Kevin let the sentence drop when he registered Jennifer's look of self-righteous rage. "Okay, okay. Enough of that. The point is, she didn't interest me, her sex drive did."

"Kevin, what's your point? I was chopped liver? Thank you once more for boosting my morale."

He laughed, knowing she didn't believe that for a minute. "No way, sweetheart. Making love to you was like making love to an angel. I felt tied to you, and that was scary. I felt trapped being engaged—not to *you*—but to the idea of commitment. Brenda offered freedom and fun to go along with it. Seemed appealing at the time, but I'm changing. I want more than something casual or replaceable when it comes to relationships."

Looking at him deeply she tried to gauge his honesty. "Is that why you got so mad at Mark after the funeral?"

Kevin answered promptly. "Yes. You're exactly the type of woman he always wanted. It amazes me that he didn't see that before. You two are perfect together. For some reason, that really ticked me off. I wondered why *we* couldn't have been that way. Why *I* haven't found something like you and Mark share together."

"Because you're not Mark."

Kevin treated her to a glare. "Who's chopped liver now, sweetheart?"

"Not you." She smiled. "You're Kevin. You're a lot of things Mark isn't."

"A heathen?"

A feeling, secretive and sexy—delightfully feminine, slid through her. It was Mark, his spirit touching her soul. She couldn't repress that sensuous reaction, despite the upset of hearing Samantha's voice on what was supposed to be Mark's telephone.

"Oh, you might be surprised." Quickly glossing the comment, she said, "You're free-spirited. Mark isn't. He achieved a great deal of success at a young age. He takes that fact very seriously, and it's important to him that he be responsible. He's so strident about being fair and impartial, and telling the truth, that often times he won't let go and cut loose without giving it a lot of forethought. You need someone spirited enough to keep up with you."

"Maybe so. I'm taking names . . ." A comfortable silence fell between them. "You know, Jen, I think friendship really messed up the two of you."

"No it didn't. Slowed down the inevitable, perhaps, but . . ." *Our friendship has left me more confident of him,* she thought. *Better able to trust.*

*So why don't I?*

Wishing he held all the answers, Jennifer turned to Kevin. "Still, all these praises of Mark's character don't answer one very important question. Why was she in his room?"

There wasn't much he could say in response. "Lots of reasons. I'm sure they would have talked to Tom Brewer if there was a problem, or a change in rooms. If I were you, I'd check with him." In his typical, devil-may-care way, Kevin offered, "Better yet, why not take some time off and join him? You've got vacation time coming, don't you? Go to him. Hash things out together face to face. Take a lover's holiday in Los Angeles."

"Kevin, that's a provocative idea, but Mark isn't out west to get a sun tan. And the *Sentinel* needs my help right now, we're kind of busy you know. Besides, where on earth would I stay?"

"Come on, Jen, you know the ol' saying about a will and a way." He gave her a tender wink. "I owe this to the two of you, after the things I've said and done. And I have some connections in La-La Land . . ."

\* \* \*

Between Samantha and Mark, the air had been swept clear of misunderstandings. They took a charter bus to the Forum that was packed with other members of the media. This would be the second and final day of media sessions before the NBA finals began. Like yesterday, the arena was divided in half by a giant purple cloth so both teams could meet with the press at once without having to confront each other.

Walking inside, Mark took charge. "Keep tabs on the Lakers for me while I check in with Phil Jackson and see what's up for the Bulls."

Nodding, Samantha extracted a tape recorder and notepad from her shoulder bag. "Will the time frame be like it was yesterday?"

Mark surveyed the stands, which were quickly filling with members of the press corps. "Yes, the interview session is only an hour long. I'll meet you in the stands when I'm finished."

What followed was an hour of chasing "name" players and hounding them for any type of comment that would make his column for tomorrow's edition of the *Sentinel*.

The seven game series would begin tomorrow night for a two game stand before switching to Chicago stadium. Like always, when a sporting event was being covered by nearly the entire world, Mark was left wondering how many fresh descriptives he would be able to come up with to describe the two teams. Hype. Especially in Los Angeles, there was no way of avoiding it.

He spotted the Bulls players gathering at a spot on the floor of the Forum and took a seat toward the front of the stands. Taking notes on automatic, he recorded quotes and observations. And thought of Jennifer.

Mid-scribble, his pen came to an abrupt halt. He had to call her. He hadn't talked to Jennifer since leaving Chicago. Ordinarily, that wouldn't concern him because he knew she would understand the busy pace of his schedule. But especially after this morning's debacle with Kevin and Samantha on the radio, he started to feel restless about making contact with her.

His fingertips twitched. He wouldn't blame Jennifer for thinking the worst—and how could he explain that the hotel had messed up their room reservation without coming off sounding incredibly insincere. Squeezing his pen like a vise, Mark felt his dread build with a hot, steady force.

There was only one way to win back his peace of mind and find out how Jennifer was. Call her, immediately if possible. Checking his watch, he considered the time difference and figured she'd be at the paper. Mark started to fidget, wanting the assurance of talking to her.

A lover's holiday in Los Angeles. Kevin had planted a ripe seed in Jennifer's mind and she couldn't help being attracted by the idea.

But showing up in California might backfire. Would Mark resent her sudden arrival? See it as intrusion and a lack of faith? Granted, she wanted to find out what had happened this morning with Samantha. Did that translate to being overly possessive? Or distrustful?

Yes, to a degree, and she knew that frame of mind was wrong. So why was the temptation to drop everything and leave still so strong?

Jennifer went to the headquarters of the *Sentinel,* prepared to forego the possible consequences and go to L.A. She needed to hold him, skim loving fingertips against the warmth of his flesh, drench herself with his kiss.

Her boss, however, was less than enthusiastic about those plans.

"You want to *what?"* Tom stuck his pinky in his ear and wiggled it around. "I couldn't have heard you right, Meyers."

She didn't find his comedy routine at all funny. She really wanted to go now. "I'm serious, Tom. I want to take two days off—tomorrow and Monday—and fly to L.A."

Taken aback, he looked her right in the eye. "You want to fly to L.A.?"

"Yes."

Resting his chin in the cup of his hand, Tom regarded her quietly for a moment, as though she were a visitor from another planet and he had no idea how to communicate with her.

"I assume this trip has nothing to do with watching your home team do some slam dunks at the Forum."

Straight on, Jennifer answered, "You're right. This trip is in no way professional. It's strictly personal."

"Mark?"

"Mark."

Tom didn't react except to continue watching her. Finally he asked, "Why can't this wait a week until he gets back?"

"I can't really answer that. All I can say is that I have the time coming, and I'd like to use it."

Looking bemused, Tom scratched his chin. "Is there any particular reason why you couldn't touch base with Mark using a *telephone*, Jen? It would be a hell of a lot cheaper, and easier on me. I'm already short handed because of finals and I need you here right now."

"Understood. Flattering, even. But I've checked the upcoming schedule. The Cubs and Sox are off Friday and Monday respectively. That helps. There's nothing big in the hopper this weekend—you'd survive." Cajoling him further, she prodded, "Right . . . ?"

"I've always found it difficult to argue with logic," Tom muttered. "But I *am* your boss, Jennifer. As your boss, I have every right to question your motives in wanting to join a fellow employee for a non-professional reason while they're on the road, putting together an important series of reports for this newspaper."

"True." Holding her breath, Jennifer gave him a level look, trying to be as smooth as possible. "And as your employee I've never given you cause to doubt my judgment. I won't start now."

"Then I won't interfere," Tom concluded with obvious effort. "What you and Mark do privately is your own business, so long as it doesn't interfere with your work. Or his. You're both respected here, and trusted, so although I have severe doubts, there's no firm reason for me to say no."

If discretion had allowed, Jennifer would have hugged the man. She knew how hard it must be for him to stay out of the situation.

During the course of their conversation, she hadn't asked for a status report on the *Sentinel* crew in Los Angeles and that omission was deliberate. This morning's phone call wasn't important to her anymore.

During the past few hours, Jennifer had discovered the faith she needed. Perhaps this newfound liberation had taken place because she had come upon one of her worst fears and faced it squarely. *Samantha Malone in his hotel room.*

Maybe this morning's phone call had been a simple mix up. Miscommunication. She could have called his hotel room immediately this morning and questioned him about Samantha. She could have heard his explanations and been assured. But would that assurance have been worth the terrible aftertaste of not showing him trust?

Regardless, she was going to give Mark what he most deserved—unquestioning love.

Returning to the conversation at hand, Jennifer said, "You won't regret the latitude you've given me, Tom."

His eyes narrowed. "I better not, Jen. I'm putting a lot of faith in you." Following a pause he ended with, "Have a nice weekend."

But his words, Jennifer knew, weren't a wish. They were a warning.

# Fourteen

At home on her lunch hour, Jennifer discovered a frantic message on her recording machine from Mark.

"Hi, Face. I called the paper and found out you had gone home for lunch. Now I miss you here. This is *not* turning out to be my day. I'll get a hold of you later. Hope everything is okay in Chicago. Bye."

What double meaning! The cadence of his voice made Jennifer laugh because he sounded like a man condemned. Jennifer could hear the echoes of doubt and uncertainty.

Ignoring Mark's message, she called the airport and discovered the first available flight to L.A. wasn't scheduled to leave O'Hare until mid-day tomorrow. At that piece of news, she felt her excitement ebb.

No amount of name dropping or wrangling helped her get an earlier leave time either, so she surrendered the fight with reluctance and booked a seat. Her call to the airport concluded, Jennifer sat on the padded chrome stool of her breakfast nook and tapped the phone receiver with a restless fingernail.

She wanted to check in with Mark, just to hear his voice and find out what was happening in Los Angeles, but she resisted. She would treat this trip like a spur of the moment, romantic rendezvous. Talking to him on the phone would be a dead give away that she had plans afoot, so, difficult though it would be, Jennifer planned on avoiding Mark until they were face to face in California.

This time there would be no mistake. She wouldn't give Mark the impression that she didn't believe in him.

Beneath her hand, the phone began to ring, jarring her thoughtful repose. "Hello?"

"Hi, Jen, it's Kevin. Are you going to go?"

She smiled at his zestful enthusiasm. "Yes. You're a scoundrel, though, and if Tom Brewer knew about your influence in my wanting to go to L.A., he'd gladly dangle you from the Sears Tower by your toes."

"That's all I wanted to know. I'll call you later."

"Woa . . . woa . . . Kevin, what in the world has gotten in to you?" She could have sworn she heard him chuckle affectionately.

"Fifteen years worth of friendship. Mark deserves this, and I owe him." Before Jennifer could protest, or say anything at all, Kevin ended gruffly, "I'll call you later with your hotel information."

"But *how?*"

"Bye, Jen."

And the line went dead.


". . . Hi, this is Jennifer. I can't come to the phone right now, but if you leave your name, number and the time that you called . . ."

Mark now knew what it meant to die a thousand deaths.

He cursed vehemently, slamming down the phone of his hotel suite in frustration. This time he disconnected the call before receiving an annoying beep, or further instructions from the scratchy, mechanical sound of Jennifer's voice. During the past several hours he had tried unsuccessfully to make contact with her.

First Jennifer's lunch hour had interfered, then she had been tied up in a production meeting. After calling back one last time, and finding out she had left the offices of the *Sentinel* for the day, Mark had tried one last time to reach Jennifer at home with a typical lack of timing luck.

Making matters worse, he had to report to the Forum for game one of the Bulls-Lakers game. By the time the game ended, it would be too late to call her again, so for now Mark had to settle for an unsuccessful round of phone tag and try again in the morning.

What must she be thinking? Had she listened to Kevin's morning show? Heard Samantha's voice when she expected to hear his? Uncertainty was driving him nuts, and he had no idea what he would come up against if Jennifer had misunderstood, drawn the wrong conclusions, and let her anger boil up over the period of an entire day.

Her trust was extremely tenuous right now. The thought of it being ruined was wearing down his normally calm demeanor.

"Damn it, Jen," he lamented aloud, "what's going on back home?"

Before leaving the hotel, Mark did a double check of his brief case, tallying his supply of cassette tapes, notebooks and pens. Satisfied with his stock for the upcoming game, Mark hitched his portable computer over his shoulder and left for the sports arena, but his heart was laden with worry.

"A jump shot at the buzzer . . . three point range for Michael Jordan . . . and it's . . . NO GOOD! No Good! The Bulls face game two tomorrow night at a one game deficit, losing the first game of the NBA finals by a single, unmerciful point!"

From his seat at the front press desk, Mark heard the dejected wail of the television commentator. The final buzzer had just sounded and he watched the Bulls players file past, most of them wearing dazed expressions, their bodies shimmering with sweat, and even blood.

He already had his headline. *Heartbreak*. From there, his thoughts for tomorrow's column stalled, replaced by images of Jennifer. Repeatedly he tried to focus on writing his account of the basketball game. Repeatedly the attempts failed.

*If only he knew what was going on back home.*

"She's *what?*"

"On vacation. She'll be back Tuesday."

Mark heard Kylie Masterson's explanation for why Jennifer wasn't at work the next morning, but he couldn't believe it. "When did she decide to do this? I didn't know anything about a vacation."

"Hey, don't ask me, Abington. I'm in the dark myself. All I know is when I asked Tom where Jennifer was, he only said she was taking a few days off."

Tuesday. He didn't know where she was and he wouldn't be able to reach her until *Tuesday*. What had gotten in to her? She had never mentioned the need for a break from work. Especially when the *Sentinel,* and indeed all of Chicago, was involved with finals madness.

What was going on?

Following that shock, Mark had no choice but to report to the Forum and do his job, chatting up the Bulls players about last night's loss and hopes for a rebound in tonight's second game.

But his thought process lacked even a semblance of intensity and resolve. He could only ask himself, over and over again, where on earth Jennifer was, and why she had disappeared without a trace.

Mark's afternoon went no better. At times, when intensity and the prospect of competition closed in around Michael Jordan the man could be absolutely impossible to deal with. Unreachable.

Frustrated, needing an interview with "His Airness" before tonight's deadline, Mark returned to the hotel reception desk and asked for messages, praying he'd hear from Jennifer. His voice and manner were terse because he didn't really expect to. She had vanished, and he couldn't figure out why.

*Damn it all,* he thought, *She'll hear about this. I've got a job to do. People in Chicago want to touch base with the Bulls' players. Michael in particular. He should be willing to grant one short interview to a hometown boy. Usually I'd have enough finesse to snare that interview, but I can't even think about it. I'm worried sick about Jennifer.*

"There's just one message, Mr. Abington. An envelope."

"What? A letter? There must be a mistake. I haven't been here long enough to get . . ."

"It was a personal delivery," the clerk inserted.

The receptionist handed Mark a pale pink envelope with a perfect white rose taped across the front.

He smiled broadly, the frustrations of the day, and his worries about Jennifer, evaporating like useless steam. Pinning his lower lip, he slit the envelope open and stepped to the side so he could read the message.

Mark:

I heard Kevin's program yesterday morning and I recognized Samantha's voice when she picked up the phone. I understand she was in your room, but do you know what? I don't care. *I trust you.*

Love always,
Your Admirer
P.S. Been to the bar yet?

No. And that's exactly where he wanted to go anyway. Lifting his briefcase, Mark went to the atrium style bar that adjoined the main lobby of the hotel. He found Jennifer immediately.

But she hadn't spotted him yet. His heart pounded in his chest, swelling, making him realize clearly that this woman belonged with him forever. The fiend.

Stepping up to her from behind, he could smell the lingering traces of her perfume. He smiled.

Lifting her hair quickly, he nipped at her neck and whispered in her ear, "You forgot the perfume on your note, Face. I missed that."

Jennifer gave a start, then beamed him the most beautiful, bewitching smile of welcome he'd ever seen.

"Hi," she greeted softly.

Sweet and shy. Mark loved that facet of her personality as much as the part of her that prompted sudden, unexpected arrivals when he needed her the most, the utter abandon of their love making, the sensuousness of her secret admirer tactics.

"Welcome to Los Angeles," he reciprocated in a low voice.

Mark's eyes sparkled, teased and enticed. Jennifer felt her stomach start to flutter with those familiar feelings of desire and longing. Her skin heated up. Toying with the stem of her wineglass, her eyes never strayed from his. "Are you angry?"

He laughed in a growling kind of way, and tugged gently on the tie of her blouse to bring her close. "As far as I'm concerned, if love were bubbles, Face, this place would look like the Lawrence Welk show."

She laughed with genuine joy and passion. Mark joined in, burying his fingers in the full, thick waves of her hair. "I'm glad you're here," he murmured.

She glazed her fingertips lightly down the front of his silk tie. "I have to admit, I got pretty mad yesterday."

Levity took its leave. "I'll bet. I thought you might recognize Sam's voice, but you were unavailable for consultation."

She blinked beguilingly. "Was I?"

He growled at her, then continued with a grin. "I've tried calling you about half a dozen times during the past twenty-four hours and you drove me crazy."

"Well I must say, I've admired her voice many times, but never over the radio, or in the context of sharing a room with the man I love."

There was no accusation in her voice. As a matter of fact, her eyes sparkled in a teasing way. Obviously she wanted to understand, though, so Mark explained. "I warn you, Jen, it's like an episode of *I Love Lucy.*"

"Tough day at the chocolate factory?"

"We checked in at the hotel, following a flight from hell, only to discover the hotel—and I emphasize that, Face—*the hotel* had made a mistake and assigned *Sam* Malone and *Mark* Abington to the same room."

She tried to keep herself from chuckling but couldn't. "They thought Sam was a man?"

Mark nodded. "She about strangled the receptionist. We started to unpack but didn't want to spend the week sharing quarters. I moved in with our staff photographer, and Kevin got the wrong room—Samantha's room—when he called."

"Um-hum." Playfully doubtful, Jennifer kept watching him. She'd never ever get tired of looking at his face. "The phone call."

"Sammie thinks fast on her feet, I'll give her that. She got rid of him in a blazing hurry."

"Just call me Ethel."

They spun in unison, facing Samantha, who had stepped up midway through Mark's explanation. Jennifer went crimson and Mark laughed. "Back me up on this, Malone, or you've had it."

Sitting next to Jennifer, she affirmed, "He speaks the truth, Jen. I only wish you would have done the same thing when I confronted you about your relationship."

Quietly, Jennifer regarded the woman. True enough. Samantha had deserved that much. But she had been so damned afraid of giving Mark leeway. "I know that now, and I'm sorry."

Samantha shrugged. "That's okay. I was a royal buttinski, and I hear you've been down a rocky road before. Still, I would have understood. I've been on the receiving end of rather blunt pain myself."

"I'm learning," Jennifer answered, offering a hand of truce. "Forgive and forget?"

Samantha smiled, shaking her hand. "You bet." She looked past Jennifer, to Mark. "Eh, Abington, how does an 8 P.M. one on one with Michael Jordan sound?"

He gaped. "Like a miracle. What are you talking about? He's tight as a wire. There's no getting to the man . . ."

"Unless you work on the coach instead of the player, throwing around names like Tom Brewer, and past book alliances—that kind of thing."

"Classic manipulation." Mark grinned, saluting her with a nod.

"Classic." Samantha stood. "If you need a place to stay, Jen, I've got an extra bed. Let me know if you need it."

"Yeah, Face, where are you staying? How did you get accommodations?"

"Through Kevin."

Samantha looked amazed. "Who is this Kevin guy? He's certainly piqued my interest during the past few days."

All Jennifer could do was shake her head. "Don't ask any more outside of that, because I don't know how he did it. I'm at a small bed and breakfast about five miles from here."

Samantha left soon afterward, and Mark moved close, sifting through her hair again, enjoying its texture. "If you're at a cozy, romantic sounding bed and breakfast, then so am I. God have I missed you."

"Me, too." She touched him as well, stroking the firm line of his jaw. But then she laughed, thinking of everything they had gone through. Friends. Lovers. Smoothing out the troubled waters of past fear and rejection.

Giving Mark a saucy look, Jennifer started to hum the theme music from *I Love Lucy*. With all due respect, Lucille Ball couldn't hold a candle to this one. Sometimes real life was twice as weird as anything on TV. And equally as happy in the end.

Mark laughed as well and pulled her close. He delved into a satiny soft, probing kiss that sent shivers down her spine, murmuring, "Aw, Luuuzeee . . ."